Christmas at
SUGAR SAND INN

SUGAR SAND BEACH
BOOK 5

LEIGH DUNCAN

Christmas at Sugar Sand Inn
Sugar Sand Beach Series, Book #5

Digital ISBN: 978-1-944258-32-0
Print ISBN: 978-1-944258-33-7
Gardenia Street Publishing

Published in the United States of America

Welcome Back to Sugar Sand Beach!

Escape to Sugar Sand Beach with best friends Michelle, Reggie, Nina and Erin for a second chance at all life has to offer.

Welcome to Christmas at the Sugar Sand Inn! Michelle and her friends have replaced the welcome sign on the front gate with one that reads "Closed for the Holidays." The four women deserve a little break after spending the summer working non-stop to convert the house Michelle inherited from her birth mother into an inn. The past three months they've definitely been thrilled—and maybe a little over-whelmed—by the influx of guests who have alternately charmed and confounded them. Now with a wedding in the works, it's no wonder the four friends need some time to kick back, help themselves to a glass of the inn's signature cocktail and enjoy the warm winter breezes that blow off the Gulf.

Of course, no holiday would be complete without a few problems. A tight housing market makes it difficult for Erin and her fiancé to find a house to rent. Meanwhile Michelle, Reggie and Nina prepare a very special surprise for the newlyweds. Unexpected arrivals complicate matters, and soon every room of the "closed" inn is filled to overflowing. Despite the problems, laughter rings throughout the halls, and good smells drift from the kitchen where Chef Nina and her team whip up holiday treats and one very special wedding cake.

Join Nina, Michelle, Reggie and Erin as they enjoy the new lives they've built in Sugar Sand Beach, where fresh opportunities for life, love and happiness are as limitless as the blue Florida skies.

One

Michelle

*W*e had *such* a lovely time. Now you do have our reservations for next year, don't you?" Cheri Jordon studied Michelle over the top of the designer sunglasses she'd perched on the tip of her nose.

"Yes, ma'am. They're in my computer. I've emailed them to you and also attached a copy to your receipt." Michelle pointed to one corner of the paperwork the departing guest had tucked into the fashionable bag she'd slung over one arm.

"You've thought of everything. After this week, I shouldn't be at all surprised." Cheri leaned forward and let her voice drop to a whisper as if she were sharing a secret. "Frankly, I wasn't sure what to expect—the inn being so

1

new and all—but we were pleasantly surprised from the moment we arrived. John especially appreciated having someone on the premises to take him fishing. He'll be bragging to all his friends about the monster red he caught. I loved the quiet nooks and being able to take long walks along the shore. It was almost like having our own private beach. I'm already looking forward to next year."

Michelle gave the woman a warm smile. According to their guest, Cheri and John planned a weeklong getaway in the Panhandle area each year. They'd given the Sugar Sand Inn and Cafe a chance only after the place they usually stayed changed hands. "We'd love it if you'd leave a comment on our website or give us a good review on Yelp." After only three months in business, the Sugar Sand Inn and Cafe already had dozens of five-star reviews on the popular travel site, but another positive rating never hurt.

"I'll do that as soon as we get home." Toying with the diamond bracelet on her right wrist, Cheri sent a wistful glance toward the stairs as if wishing she didn't have to leave at all. The watch on her other wrist dinged. Almost deliberately, she straightened. "That's John. He's bringing the car around. I'll have to jet. I simply must snag a couple of those delicious cinnamon rolls from the cafe and some coffee for the road. Then we're off."

Michelle nodded, confident that Nina had set aside enough rolls for Cheri and John despite their late checkout. Sure enough, not ten minutes passed before the woman reappeared, this time carrying two cups of coffee in a cardboard tray with a bulging paper bag balanced on top. Michelle held the door for her and watched as the ever-attentive John sprang from the car to assist his wife. It took no time at all for Cheri to get settled into the passenger seat or for John to take his place behind the wheel. As their rental car headed down the graveled driveway, Michelle leaned against the doorframe and sighed.

"Was that the last of them?" Erin emerged from the long hall into the entryway.

"Yep." The roomy sedan turned onto the main road that ran in front of the inn. In seconds, it rounded a corner and disappeared. "The Sugar Sand Inn is officially closed for the holidays. Time to relax." Not that they'd exactly be taking it easy for the next three weeks. Not with Christmas in a mere fourteen days, to say nothing of the wedding that would follow. Certainly not with Zeke and his crew descending on the house tomorrow to begin transforming the unfinished turret into a sumptuous hideaway.

She glanced at Erin. As activity director for the inn, Erin had spent countless hours in kayaks and canoes, on bicycles or hiking the many local trails, and her skin had darkened into a golden tan. Despite an ever-present ball cap, the sun had lightened Erin's thick, blond hair over the seven months since they'd moved to Sugar Sand Beach, but her eyes remained as clear as they'd always been. Had her friend guessed the surprise wedding present she and Nina and Reggie had been planning? Surely, if Erin had tumbled onto the secret the rest of them had been keeping, Michelle would have seen suspicion in her friend's hazel eyes. Or in the smile that hadn't wavered since the night Ron had proposed.

"What do you have planned for the afternoon? Wedding preparations?" she asked. Even though Erin and Ron were having a simple ceremony and reception with only their closest friends and family in attendance, she had an endless list of details to arrange. She'd make a beautiful bride, thought Michelle.

"Nope." Erin's smile deepened into a full-fledged grin. "Reggie's helping me put together the gift baskets for our Christmas party on Tuesday." Once a week, retirees from Sugar Sand Beach and the surrounding areas gathered at the inn for a day of cards and board games. This week's event would be the final one of the year, and Erin planned to make it a memorable occasion. "How about you? Do you and Dave have a hot date?"

"Ha ha." Michelle faked a laugh. Much as she'd like to see the tall, distinguished-looking attorney, the law offices of Rollins & Rollins would remain open until Christmas Eve before closing for the holidays. "We're both busy right now, but we're planning some day trips for the week before New Year's. Biloxi. Thomasville." Both destinations were an easy two to three hours' drive.

"No overnight trips?" Erin wiggled her eyebrows.

Michelle felt her cheeks warm. Ever the gentleman, Dave had honored her request to take things slow. Lately, though, the kisses they shared had stirred a deepening desire for something she'd never considered a possibility in the year following her husband's death. Were they ready to take things to the next level?

She shook her head, both in answer to Erin's question and her own. Aloud, she said, "No. I'm not ready for that kind of relationship." *But one day, maybe.*

"So if you're not going to see Sugar Sand Beach's favorite attorney, what are you going to do with the rest of your day?" Erin wanted to know.

"Well, first, I'm going to take a little walk down to the front gate and hang up the 'Closed' sign." Much as she'd loved running the inn these past three months, Michelle was looking forward to the four of them having the house all to themselves for the next couple of weeks. "Then I have a meeting with Zeke to finalize the plans for the turret before he and his crew start work on it tomorrow. After that, I have some admin stuff to catch up on." From paychecks to tax forms, an astounding amount of paperwork went into the smooth running of the inn.

"Sounds like we'll both have a busy afternoon. We're still meeting on the porch at five, though, aren't we?"

"Yes, and I, for one, can't wait. It's been ages."

Were the others looking forward to this evening's get-together as much as she was? Michelle thought they probably were. When she and Nina, Erin and Reggie had first arrived in Sugar Sand Beach, they'd gathered on the porch at the end of each day. As the sun slowly sank, they sipped iced tea or punch and shared a snack or two while they brought each other up to date with all they'd accomplished, as well as their plans for the days ahead. Sitting there, letting the cool Gulf breezes wash over them, listening to the waves roll ashore on the beach a mere hundred yards away, had been a little slice of heaven.

It was also one they couldn't deny to their paying customers. So once the inn's first official guests had checked in, Michelle had moved the foursome's daily get-togethers into the office off the kitchen. But from now until the first of the year, they'd take full advantage of the opportunity to sit on the porch and enjoy the scenery.

Michelle reached beneath the table they used as the reception desk and pulled out a large piece of driftwood. The sign Reggie had painted announced to one and all that the inn was not open for guests. Eager to begin their first break since the grand opening, Michelle tucked the board under her arm and headed for the front gate.

As Nina filled tall glasses with Gulf Coast Sunset, the inn's signature drink, Michelle settled against the cushions of her favorite rattan chair.

The sun had dropped below the waters of the Gulf only minutes earlier. The clouds gathered on the distant horizon were still ablaze with reds and golds. She traced her fingers along the edges of the light cardigan she'd worn over a long-sleeved cotton shirt and wool slacks. The extra layer was all she needed, and she relished the difference between December in Sugar Sand Beach and her old home in Virginia, where by now, she'd already be wearing a heavy coat and gloves whenever she stepped outside.

"It's hard to believe it's nearly Christmas and we're still able to meet out here," she said.

"I am loving this Florida weather," Reggie said. "Do you realize how lucky we are that we're still getting vegetables out of the garden this late in the season?" Although the green beans and tomatoes were long gone, she'd carried an armload of lettuce and kale into the kitchen this very morning. She swiped a crab puff off the tray Nina had placed on the table. "Ummmm. These are so good, Nina."

"Ethan brought us two pounds of already-picked crab meat this morning." Nina's whole face lit up. "I swear. That boy sure knows his way to my heart. It was such a treat, I had to share it with everyone."

"I'm glad he's working out for you." Michelle

crossed her ankles. "I know you had reservations about hiring someone so young and inexperienced." What little Ethan had known about working in a restaurant he'd learned at culinary school.

"He's turned into quite the capable young cook," Nina acknowledged. "He did a great job filling in for Viola the week she had to take off when Dimella and Malcolm got the flu. In fact, I've been so impressed by him that I'm making him my line cook for the dinner service." Response to the cafe had been so positive that they'd all agreed to extend the cafe's hours until nine on Friday and Saturday nights beginning in January.

"Really?" Erin quirked an eyebrow. "I thought Viola would take that spot."

"I offered it to her. She turned it down." Nina took a sip of her drink. "Until the kids go off to college, she wants to spend the evenings at home with them."

"Can't say as I blame her for that," Michelle said. Dimella and Malcolm were both in middle school. When her twins were that age, it had taken constant vigilance to stay one step ahead of them. She hated to think of the trouble they'd have gotten into if she'd left them to their own devices at night. Keg parties in the basement?

Joyriding in their father's car? Ambulances and solemn-faced policemen at the door?

She swallowed hard. Thank goodness, they'd outgrown that phase.

She'd always be grateful that she'd been able to stay home with the kids when they were younger. As they reached their teen years, her focus had shifted to helping them become independent young adults. A task she'd accomplished, although lately she wondered if she'd been a little too good at her job. Especially this year, when both Aaron and Ashley had decided to spend the Christmas holidays with friends instead of joining her in Florida. She swirled her drink and took a sip. She cast about, searching for a different subject. As usual, Erin seemed to read her mind.

"You really outdid yourself with the decorations," her friend said with a nod to the ornaments and lights that hung from the tree on the porch. "The house looks really festive."

"Someone might have mentioned a Christmas wedding." Glad to think of something besides her children, Michelle waggled her eyebrows. "We can't very well have one of those without hanging some garlands and decorating a few trees."

"A tree in every room, though? Don't you

think that might be a bit much?" Erin asked.

"Not every room," Michelle corrected. Though she'd placed trees in each parlor and the dining room, she hadn't seen any point in decorating the guest suites that would remain empty through Christmas.

"Well, I love them. So does Hope," Reggie insisted. "We had great fun the other day looking at all the decorations. She loved the Santa Clauses in the library. I swear her eyes got as big as saucers when she saw them. I think she wanted to take them all home with her."

"There's nothing like seeing the magic of Christmas through a child's eyes," Michelle said wistfully. Before her own children could crowd her thoughts again, she turned to the others.

"We've had a lot of fun these last few months, haven't we?" she asked. "I think the thing that surprised me most of all was how smoothly things have gone. Quite frankly, I was afraid people would be rapping on my door at all hours, complaining that their room was too hot or too cold or that the toilet was plugged up."

"It really hasn't been too bad, has it?" Erin propped her feet on the edge of Reggie's chair. "We've had some wonderful guests. My favorites were the Hamptons." The family of four had spent an entire week at the inn just before

Thanksgiving. "It was neat watching Genna learn how to launch her own kayak and helping Kevin land his first fish on a fly rod." The pre-teens had signed up for kayaking and fishing lessons every day. "How about everyone else? Favorites? Guests you'd like to vote off the island?"

"That gator definitely gets the boot." Reggie swore softly. She'd spotted the six-footer cruising around the pond at the back of the property two months ago. "I'm just thankful Ethan's dad was able to catch it before one of our guests wandered too close or one of their dogs decided to go swimming." With Mr. Pibbs, Nina's cat, in residence, they'd encouraged guests to take advantage of the inn's pet-friendly policies. A few had.

"I was glad he took the meat as payment for trapping the gator and disposing of it." Rather than pay the small fee for removal of the nuisance gator, Michelle had bartered goods for services. "I figured no one here would eat it. Right?"

Reggie held her nose. "Oh gross. No thanks." They'd all tried gator meat once, and that once had been enough.

"I certainly wouldn't serve it in the cafe. It's too gamy-tasting, and the texture's just…off. We'd be comping meals left and right."

"You don't have to do that too often, do you?" Reggie lifted an eyebrow.

Nina shrugged. "We have had the occasional disgruntled customer, of course—that's normal in the restaurant business. But our most frequent complaint has been that we don't serve beer or wine. Those will taper off after we get our liquor license this month."

Michelle nodded. She and Nina had filled out the appropriate applications together.

The chef sampled one of the crab puffs. Waving it through the air like a baton, she said, "On the plus side, I've loved watching Jack romance Ruth Bees." The octogenarians had been secretly dating for several months now. "Seeing those two together makes me feel all warm and squishy inside."

"You should see them during Senior Days. They spar just as much now as they used to, but every once in a while, Ruth will give Jack such a look." Erin placed her hand over her heart. "I wonder if they'll tie the knot."

"That's one wedding the entire town would turn out for," Michelle said. She scanned the group. Within just a few days, Erin would walk down the aisle to marry Ron. Nina and Zeke spent every spare moment together. Though Reggie and Chris weren't officially dating, she suspected things would change once Reggie's divorce became final. As for herself, she'd never thought herself capable of falling in love again, but that's exactly what she was doing, wasn't it? Closing her eyes, she pictured a parade of brides walking down the stairs of the inn to join the men they loved.

Reggie studied the liquid in her glass for several seconds before she asked, "How does Maggie feel about the two of them?"

Michelle started. She cleared her throat. She'd let her thoughts drift too far into the future. Out of the four of them, only Erin planned on marrying any time soon. She put her daydreams aside to focus on Reggie's question. "Maggie knows about her uncle's relationship with Ruth." In the small town of Sugar Sand Beach, news spread from one end of the town's grapevine to the other faster than a lightning strike, and Jack had been spotted leaving Ruth's house in the mornings on several occasions. "She's as happy as the rest of us that he's found someone."

"It was the inn that brought them together. That's what I'm happy about." Erin brushed her hair behind one ear.

"How do you figure?" Reggie wanted to know.

"Well, if it hadn't been for Senior Days, they might still be alone."

Michelle gave that idea a moment's thought before she agreed. "She's right, you know. Jack and his buddies hung out at Maggie's Diner every day. They never went to the Community Center like Ruth and her friends." Tuesdays at the inn had brought the two groups together.

"An unexpected side benefit of running the prettiest place in town." Nina sipped her drink.

Michelle stretched, trying to work a sudden tightness out of her shoulders as her thoughts turned to a topic they needed to address. The time had come to evaluate where they stood and how they wanted to proceed. Shortly before their first guests arrived, she and Erin, Reggie and Nina had formed a partnership that gave them each an equal say in the inn's future. As much as she wanted to keep the doors open, Michelle couldn't make that decision on her own. Did her friends feel the same way she did, or did they want to sell the property and move on to something else?

She coughed softly. "I don't know about the rest of you, but I've enjoyed the last few months more than I thought possible. I mean, I knew running the inn and cafe would mean a lot of work—"

"It is that!" Nina exclaimed, though her eyes twinkled merrily.

"Yes, it is," Michelle agreed. "But I've enjoyed meeting our guests and seeing to their needs."

"I'll say this…" Nina set her glass on the table and leaned back. "Having my own restaurant is everything I ever dreamed it could be and more."

As Michelle turned to the youngest member of their group, she noticed that Reggie's expression had tightened the way it did whenever she thought of the husband who'd walked out on her marriage eight months earlier.

"I was a mess when Sam and I first decided to divorce," Reggie admitted. "Spending time planting and bringing new things to life has been very healing for me." She shifted in her chair. Her features lost their pinched look. "I've found my true calling. Having the garden and being responsible for the landscaping is exactly what I want to do."

"Same here." Erin played with the diamond on the third finger of her left hand. "I'm right where I want to be, doing what I want to do."

"So, what do you think?" Relieved at what she was hearing, Michelle put the question to the rest of the group. "Do you see yourselves running the inn and cafe for the rest of your lives?"

Erin squinted. "Well...maybe not forever," she hedged.

"But probably for the next twenty or thirty years," Reggie added.

"Yeah." Erin, whose feet still rested on Reggie's chair, prodded her sister's leg with her toes. "What she said."

"How about you, Nina?" Michelle turned to the chef. "You're being awfully quiet."

"That's because I don't have anything to add. I can't imagine doing anything else with my life."

"Then it's settled," Michelle said as the tightness in her shoulders evaporated. "We'll continue to operate the Sugar Sand Inn and Cafe for at least another decade or two. Maybe longer."

Picking up their drinks, they leaned forward. Glass clinked as they toasted the future of the inn and cafe that had given each of them a new purpose in life.

Two

Erin

*E*rin fussed with the white beard Ron had pulled down over his cheeks. Careful not to knock his wig askew, she brushed a few of the white curls away from the wire-rimmed glasses he'd pushed up his nose. Stepping back, she eyed their handiwork. Even with the pillow he'd tucked beneath the bright red suit, Ron looked too slim and trim to make a convincing Santa. But that was all right. He wasn't trying to pull the wool over the eyes of a skeptical seven-year-old. He'd agreed to dress as jolly old Saint Nick and pass out presents to the attendees at the Senior Day holiday party. His audience today would be a lot more forgiving than most children.

She picked up the Naughty and Nice list she'd written on heavy parchment using the calligraphy skills she'd learned during a lengthy stay in Japan. She scanned the office desk. "Where are the lumps of coal? The candy?"

Ron patted the burlap sack that hung from his wrist by a cord. "I have them right here," he said. He cleared his throat and pitched his voice in a lower, more Santa-like tone. "Right here," he repeated.

"I'll trade you." Erin held up the list.

"For a kiss?" Ron slipped one arm around her waist.

At his touch, Erin melted against him. Considering the rather large pillow between them and the two-foot-long elf shoes she wore, it wasn't easy. Nevertheless, they gave it their best effort. Ron's whiskers tickled, and she giggled, ending the kiss much too soon.

"Just two more weeks." Ron waggled the furry white eyebrows that had come with the Santa suit.

"Can't wait," Erin said a little breathlessly. She paused. She'd been pleasantly surprised when Ron had suggested they spend their honeymoon at her cottage in Key West. Given his recent interest in travel, she'd thought for sure he'd want to fly to Tahiti or Bora-Bora. But he hadn't, and she'd decided to save that idea for their fifth wedding anniversary.

Now if they could only find a place to live after the honeymoon, everything would be perfect. True, they planned to build a house, but even if all went well with the construction—and with Zeke in charge, she was pretty sure it would—it'd be a year before they could move in. Which meant they'd have to rent in the meantime and, thanks to the annual influx of winter residents, finding an apartment or a house was proving tougher than they'd anticipated. Ron, bless his heart, had volunteered to find them a place, but long-term rentals in Sugar Sand Beach were proving to be scarcer than hens' teeth.

"Any luck finding a house or an apartment?" she asked. If she didn't know better, she'd say everyone in town had joined a nefarious plot to prevent them from renting a place. But that was silly. Wasn't it?

Sadly, Ron shook his head. "I'm supposed to check in with Nellie later today." As soon as word of their engagement spread as far as the grocery store—which took all of two minutes—Gus had recommended his sister-in-law, a Realtor with Tri-State Realty. "So far, we haven't found anything suitable. I thought I had a lead on a place—a double-wide Ruth Bees's late husband used as a hunting cabin. But she told me earlier that she'd agreed to lease the land it sits on to a group of deer hunters. Besides, it sounds pretty rustic."

Erin pictured a moldering trailer set in the woods. For the sake of romance, she told herself she'd be okay roughing it for a year as long as she and Ron were together. But no. It was one thing to pitch a tent under the stars in Alaska. Quite another to live without electricity or running water in Florida. "Yeah, that's not really my cup of tea. But where are we going to live?" Time was running short. Two weeks until the wedding plus a two-week honeymoon gave them less than a month to find a place.

"Don't worry." Ron chucked her under her chin. "I want a sturdy roof over our heads and air-conditioning as much as you do. If we have to, we'll get a room in the inn for the year. But I'll keep looking."

"In that case..." Erin ran a hand over her green-and-red elf costume. "Are you ready?"

"Ho, ho, ho!" Ron patted his "belly."

"Let's do this." She smiled.

Ron's eyes twinkled. "Ho, ho, ho! Merry Christmas!" He stomped down the hall just like they'd rehearsed. With every step, the bells Erin had sewn into the faux fur on the tops of his boots jingled.

"Ho, ho, ho!" he called, his voice lower and deeper. "Merry Christmas!"

Careful not to trip over the long, curved tips of her elf shoes, Erin followed Santa into the big parlor, where the smell of pine trees and garlands mingled with the scent of gingerbread that wafted from a tray of oven-fresh cookies on the sideboard. Surprise and laughter filled the lined faces of the men and women who normally gathered at the inn for card and board games on Tuesdays. As Santa made the rounds, greeting each one by name, their reaction to her surprise Christmas party was exactly what Erin had hoped for. Her heart softened even more for this group that had come to mean so much to her over the last three months.

She signaled Ron, who crossed to the middle of the room, where he cleared his throat. In his best Santa voice, he said, "Now listen here, boys and girls." He waited while a burst of laughter died down. "I've been watching you. I know when you've been naughty. I know when you've been nice. And I've made a list." He unfurled the parchment Erin had handed him. "Let's see, the first person here is little Ruthie Bees."

More laughter erupted. In her seat at the card table, Ruth pressed both of her hands over her mouth. Above the tips of her fingers, the wrinkles in her forehead crinkled with delight.

"According to my list, you've been a very good girl all year." Ron peered through his spectacles at Ruth. "Is that true?"

"Oh, yes, Santa." Giggling like a schoolgirl, Ruth nodded.

At Ron's "Elf Erin, will you please give Ruthie some candy?" Erin hurried to Ruth as fast as her slippery shoes would allow. Pulling a thick, peppermint candy cane from the bag, she placed it in Ruth's age-spotted hands.

Seated at the same table, Dottie waved her hand wildly. "Me, me! Do me next, Santa!"

"Harrumph." Ron cleared his throat. He and Erin shared a look.

Erin studied the woman who could be counted on to show up bearing a pot of homemade chicken noodle soup whenever someone in Sugar Sand Beach caught more than the sniffles. Teasing, she shook her finger. "Now, now, Dottie. Don't get pushy. Santa will have to move you from the Nice List to the Naughty List if you cut in line."

"Oh! I'm one of the nice ones!" Dottie slid her hands beneath the table. "I'll be good and wait my turn, Santa."

Erin gave Dottie a conspiratorial smile. Over her shoulder, she called, "Santa, I think we can give Dottie her candy now, can't we?"

When Ron agreed, Erin doled out another peppermint stick.

Ron squinted at his list. His shoulders slumped and his head drooped as he shook it. "I'm sorry to say that the next little boy on my list has misbehaved a lot this year," he said, sounding very sad. "I heard he even tricked the new waitress at Maggie's Diner into giving him two desserts."

"Oh, no!" Erin exclaimed. Letting her eyes widen, she clamped a hand over her mouth, much to the delight of their guests.

"Yes. That's right." Ron singled out the mayor's uncle. "It says here, Jack, that you've been a naughty, naughty boy. All you get from Santa this year is a lump of coal."

"That pie was worth it," Jack declared. He smacked his lips.

His actions earned the older gentleman a round of guffaws from the men seated at his table.

Discovering it was easier to slide across the hardwood floors in the awkward shoes, Erin slip-slided to the tall man who sat ramrod-straight despite his eighty-plus years on the earth. This time, she pulled a chunk of black licorice from the bag. The candy's plastic wrapper crinkled noisily as she placed it in Jack's gnarled fingers.

"Well, don't that beat all," Jack said, eyeing the candy.

Erin winked at him. The sometimes crotchety Jack had mentioned how much he loved black licorice several months ago. She'd filed that little piece of information away, saving it for just this occasion.

It took another half hour for Ron to work his way through the Naughty and Nice List. Once she'd dispensed all but a few of the candies and placed the extras in a small bowl on the sideboard, Erin sank to her knees beside the Christmas tree. One by one, she read the gift tags on the bags she and her sister had filled with personal care products, stationery and pairs of warm socks. In addition to the generic gifts, Erin had added something special for each member of the group.

Every Tuesday without fail, John had taken extra cookies from the tray on the sideboard and tucked them into the pocket of his overalls when he thought no one was looking. Today, the retired farmer beamed when he discovered a tin of cookies in the bottom of his bag. Ruth loved playing Hand-and-Foot with the rest of her friends, but whenever she took a break from the card game, she crocheted. Looking into her bag, she happily fingered the two skeins of royal blue yarn she found there. The look she sent Jack told Erin the man might just find a blue scarf with his name on it under Ruth's Christmas tree. Hazel often complained about being cold. And no wonder. The tiny woman didn't have a spare ounce of fat on her body. Erin hoped the paisley shawl tucked in with her other gifts would help Hazel stay warm, and she was delighted when the older woman immediately draped it around her shoulders.

Erin held her breath when Santa handed Jack his present. Of all the members in the tight-knit group of retirees, Jack had been the most difficult to buy for. Mostly because the man lacked for nothing. Maggie and her son, Zeke, made sure of that. True, Jack had a weakness for key lime pie. And he did love his coffee. But Maggie had limited him to one slice a day, and Jack's doctor had ordered him to switch to decaf. Other than a cup of real coffee and an extra piece of pie, Erin had never once heard Jack ask for anything. But knowing how much Ruth Bees liked ice cream, Erin had visited the small ice cream shop that had recently opened on Sugar Sand Beach's main street. There she'd purchased a gift card good for two ice cream sundaes.

Now the breath Erin had been holding slowly slipped through her lips as Jack waved the coupon at Ruth before slipping it into the bib pocket of his overalls. Erin gave herself an imaginary pat on the back. The gift card would give Jack the perfect excuse to do what he wanted to do anyway—take Ruth out on a real date.

When everyone had their gifts, Erin stood. "It's almost time for lunch, but Chef Nina has asked us to wait a few minutes before we join her." To thank the group for the extra business they'd given the cafe, Nina was treating their Senior Day guests to open-faced turkey sandwiches. "How about singing Christmas carols while we wait?" But her plan to start with "God Rest Ye Merry Gentlemen" derailed when Ruth shook her head.

"We have a little something for you, Erin," Ruth announced.

"And for Ron," Jack added.

"We all know there's going to be a wedding at the inn before the first of the year," Ruth said.

"Just a small one," Erin interrupted. She scanned the room, her expression apologetic. "You know I'd invite every one of you to the wedding, but Ron and I"—she grabbed Ron's hand—"are getting married on Christmas Day. We couldn't ask you to give up time with your own families on such an important holiday, so it's going to be a very small wedding. Just my sister and Nina and Michelle."

"Oh, honey. We wouldn't think of intruding on your special day." Ruth didn't seem the least bit concerned at being left off the guest list. "Most of us are either going out of town for the holidays or we have family coming to visit us." Around the room, white-haired heads and several bald ones bobbed up and down in agreement.

Obviously appointed spokesperson for the group, Ruth continued, "But since this is our last meeting before the new year, we wanted to throw a little surprise wedding shower for you."

Tears welled in Erin's eyes. She squeezed Ron's hand, and he squeezed hers in return. Together, they sank onto a nearby loveseat.

"Now it's not much. We pooled our money and bought something we thought you'd both enjoy." Ruth's gaze traveled to one of the men seated on the couch. "Toby, you still got that box I gave you?"

"Sure do." The portly Toby sidled over to the wall where he pulled a box wrapped in shiny white paper and adorned with a silver bow from behind the couch.

Erin shook her head. Ordinarily, she kept close tabs on the comings and goings of her charges on

Tuesdays. Flo and Frank, in particular, had a tendency to wander off on their own, and she worried that they'd venture too close to the pond out back or decide to take a swim in the ocean. But today, she'd been so focused on getting ready for Santa's appearance that Toby had been able to sneak the gift past her while she wasn't looking.

"You gotta guess what's inside," the older man said as he walked toward Erin.

The box Toby handed her was surprisingly light. She tilted it to one side and then another. Something rustled inside. "Definitely not a set of china," she joked.

"Nope. And no dishes, neither," Billy shot back.

She handed the box to Ron.

"Is it breakable?" he asked.

"No," Flo said, her voice strident.

Ron jiggled it up and down. Erin heard more rustling.

"I forget." Frank turned to the man who sat beside him. "John, what'd we get them?"

John leaned forward to stage-whisper into Frank's good ear. "Heck if I know. I just paid my five dollars and let the women figure it out."

Erin smothered a smile while she pretended to ignore the men's conversation. "It's not heavy enough to be a pot or a pan." She shot a questioning glance in Ron's direction. "Towels, maybe?"

"I don't know. It doesn't weigh much at all." He hefted the box. "I'm going to guess it's kitchen towels or a potholder."

Clearly enjoying the situation, Ruth shook her head.

"Is it...something to wear?" Erin asked tentatively.

"It could be. Care to be more specific?" Ruth asked.

"You might also say it's something to take off." Jack elbowed his pal John, who cackled like a biddy hen.

Almost as afraid of what she'd find inside the box as she was that she'd hurt someone's feelings after they'd gone to so much trouble, Erin borrowed Ron's pocket knife. She snipped the ribbon and slipped off the bow.

"Does it count if she cuts the ribbon? Or only if she breaks it?" Dottie asked no one in particular.

"Cut. Broke. No difference. They'll have a baby for sure before a year passes." A pleased look on her face, Hazel folded her arms.

Pitching her voice for Ron's ears only, Erin whispered, "Uh-uh. Ribbon or no ribbon, I'm not having a baby." She and Ron had no intention of starting a family in their mid-forties.

The paper slid easily off the box. She slipped one hesitant finger under the lid and pried it up. When nothing in a gaudy red or a sexy black met her gaze, she sighed with relief. Gingerly, she peeled back the layers of tissue. Her breath caught.

"Oh, this is lovely," she said. She grasped the sleeveless nightgown by the shoulders and held it up for the others to see. Yards of sheer, cream-colored fabric billowed from a fitted bodice.

"We wanted to get you something nice for your honeymoon. Do you like it?" Ruth asked, her voice filled with hope.

Erin held the gown to her chest. "I love it," she said, her words heartfelt. "Thank you all. Thank you so much." She scanned the room while she made eye contact with each of the regular Tuesday crowd.

By the time she finished, her phone had chimed with a text from Nina. After reading it, she carefully folded the gown back into its box. "I'm going to put this away, but in the meantime, Chef Nina would like it if you joined her in the dining room for lunch."

Chairs scraped and walkers thumped as, laughing and chatting, the group made its way out of the parlor. Beside Erin, Ron scratched idly at the fake beard. "If Santa's finished, I'd like to get out of this costume. Meet you in the cafe in a few minutes? Unless you'd like to model our gift for me?" He tapped one finger on the top of the box.

"With all these people around? I think not." Erin gave Ron's upper arm a good-natured poke. Though his crestfallen expression tempted her to reconsider, she remained resolute. The negligee would stay safely tucked away until their wedding night.

"It's just as well that I can't change your mind. I have a meeting at the marina in Destin at two to look at a fishing boat. Before I go, I want to call Nellie and see if she's found anything new for rent."

"About that." Erin lightly placed a hand on Ron's thigh. "I know we were just joking around about the pots and pans and towels earlier, but it started me thinking. I'm so used to traveling light that it never occurred to me that we'd need more than clothes and maybe a few towels. I don't have anything to set up housekeeping. No lamps. No furniture. What little I did have, I gave to Michelle for the inn. What about you? You must have had all that stuff in Houston."

"I did. But I let it all go with the house." Ron

had sold the house he'd inherited from his father, along with the outdoor sports business he'd built, shortly after he arrived in Sugar Sand Beach. "Hmmm." He tapped his chin. "What about the cottage? Is it outfitted?"

"Well, yeah." Her place in the Keys had all the usual furnishings—a coffee maker and a waffle iron, an assortment of dishware and frying pans. But because she rented the place out for the better part of the year, she'd chosen the furnishings more for durability than beauty.

Ron shrugged. "Then we'll be okay for a couple of weeks. As for the rest, we'll figure it out as we go."

"Wherever we stay," Erin cautioned, "it'd be best if we find something that's fully furnished, right down to the table linens. I'm just sayin'."

Three

Reggie

Whistling a silly Christmas song about grandma and Santa's reindeer, Reggie walked to the mailbox at the entrance to the Sugar Sand Inn and Cafe. Along the way, she couldn't help but admire her handiwork. The evenly spaced hostas and bird of paradise in the well-mulched beds on either side of the graveled driveway were a far cry from the weed-choked plants she'd spotted the day she and Erin, Michelle and Nina had first driven onto the property. Once she'd freed them from the kudzu vine that had nearly strangled them to death, the firecracker and chenille plants had thrived over the summer. Though she'd subjected both to a heavy pruning after the last blooms had fallen, she had no doubt the plants would greet their arriving guests with a showy display next spring.

At the top of the slight rise that hid the inn from passersby, Reggie turned for a look at the house that had changed her life, as well as Erin's, Michelle's and Nina's. With the hurricane season officially behind them, the storm shutters had been banished to the garage for another year. Beneath clear winter skies, sunlight sparkled off the metal roof of the two-story Queen Anne-style house. Green accents added a touch of vibrant color to the freshly painted white exterior. Red glinted from the stained-glass window above the second-floor balcony. Reggie didn't know how Michelle had managed to match the colors so precisely, but the same red hues were reflected in the garlands that outlined the porch and the cheery Christmas wreath on the front door. The house Michelle had inherited from her birth mother exuded warmth and charm, and Reggie whispered a silent prayer of thanks for the new life she was building in Sugar Sand Beach.

Still whistling, she continued on to the oversize mailbox at the end of the driveway. There, she took a key from her pocket, inserted it into the lock and swung the door aside. The dark interior was crammed full of envelopes, catalogues and other advertisements, and she began removing them. She arranged the dozens of Christmas-card-size envelopes into a neat stack and shook her head. It seemed like everyone for miles around had sent holiday greetings to the inn. The two card stands on either side of the fireplace in the family room were already filled to overflowing. She had no idea where these would go. On the mantel, maybe?

A few bills in long, white envelopes and a handful of rectangular cards promoting everything from insurance policies to retirement funds came next. She straightened the edges of furled catalogues and added them to her pile. As she did, a manila envelope slipped out from between a brochure from a popular clothing company and one touting popcorn in a variety of flavors and containers. The brown envelope had been addressed to her. Her hand stilled. The song she'd been whistling died as she read the name in the upper left corner.

Sheldon Cole.

She knew only one Sheldon—the attorney her sister had hired when Reggie had finally decided to make her separation from Sam a permanent one. Had the divorce been finalized? She counted back. Virginia law required a six-month cooling-off period before the final decree was awarded. It had been that long since she'd filed the necessary paperwork. Was this what she'd been waiting for? She shook her head. No one had mentioned a particular court date, but what else could it be?

"Merry Christmas to me." Sarcasm laced her voice as her buoyant spirits sank like stones tossed into a pond. She kicked a loose piece of gravel. It flew into the grass. Slipping the sturdy envelope to the bottom of the pile, she gritted her teeth as she pulled the rest of the mail from the box and added it haphazardly to the armload she already held.

Silently, she trudged back to the house, where she removed only the attorney's envelope before leaving the rest of the mail in a messy stack on the entryway table. Avoiding the kitchen, where, from the smell of things, Nina and Viola were baking Christmas cookies, she slipped out the front door without being seen. She took the long way around the house to the small apartment attached to the Activity Center.

Normally she could count on having the place to herself during the day while Erin was busy with the inn's guests. But the Closed sign hanging from the gate at the end of the driveway increased the odds that she'd run into her sister if she went inside. At the last minute, Reggie detoured to the garage. There, surrounded by the tools she used to maintain the five acres that had come with the house, she sank onto a folding chair. She worked one finger under the corner flap and pried the envelope open. Holding it upside down, she dumped the contents onto her lap.

She stared at the blank back of a packet of papers that had been stapled together and took a beat. When she felt she was ready, she flipped the pages over and studied the surprisingly plain header of a decree that put an end to the five-year marriage of Samuel and Regina Frank.

"What? You were expecting a royal edict on a scroll?" Hot tears stung her eyes.

She had no idea how much time passed before she heard footsteps outside.

"Reggie, you in there?" The door to the garage squeaked open. "I thought we were meeting at the pole barn to..." Chris's long legs halted in mid-stride. "Reggie?" he asked softly. "Are you okay?"

"Yeah, yeah. Just, uh, give me a minute." Her cheeks heating with embarrassment at getting caught crying, she swiped at her eyes with the backs of her hands. Not that it did a lick of good. Any fool could tell what she'd been doing, and Chris was no fool.

"Hey, this is me you're talking to. What's wrong?" Concern deepened the lines that bracketed Chris's mouth.

"It's…nothing," she said as she tried to stanch her tears.

Coming closer, Chris scooped up the papers that must have slid from her lap while she was lost in regret for a life not lived. "Oh," he said with a glance at the top page. "Your divorce." He handed the papers to her quickly, as if touching them had seared his fingers. "Sorry. I didn't mean to pry."

"It's okay. Honest." She drew in a steadying breath. "It looks like I've been divorced for ten days." She pointed to the date at the top of the first page. "Funny. I didn't even know about it. Not until this came in today's mail."

Chris's weight shifted from one foot to another. At last, he upended an empty five-gallon bucket, placed it beside Reggie and lowered himself onto the makeshift chair. "You still love him," he said with a quiet finality that carried a heavy undertone of regret.

"What?" Reggie reeled back. Whatever she'd been expecting Chris to say, that wasn't it. "No! My love for Sam died a long time ago," she insisted. Not one of the tears she'd shed had been for her ex-husband.

"You were married to him for five years," Chris pointed out. "That's a long time to be with someone you don't love."

"I'll admit, I loved him once. But every secret I uncovered about Sam killed a little bit more of my feelings for him until there was nothing left. He's a manipulative, cheating liar. Believe me, I don't miss him in the least."

"If that's true, why are you sitting all alone in the garage? Why are you crying? You're free now. I thought you'd be celebrating."

"To tell you the truth, I did, too." She hadn't expected the sense of loss that had overwhelmed her the moment she saw the attorney's return address. "When I opened the envelope and it hit me that my marriage was finally over, I—I needed a minute. It was a lot to take in."

One look at Chris's furrowed brow and she knew he didn't understand. She couldn't blame him. For a while there, she'd been confused, too. But if she and Chris had any hope of a future together, he needed to know that Sam was out of her life forever.

She took a breath. "I'd never, not in a million years, want Sam back. Still, I can't ignore the fact that, once upon a time, he was the man I planned to spend the rest of my life with. We were going to raise a family, grow old together. It took him walking out on our marriage for me to finally realize he wasn't the man I thought he was. And those dreams died. When I saw the divorce decree"—she smoothed one hand over the papers—"it all came rushing back—my hopes for a future that was never meant to be. I needed some time to mourn those dreams."

For a long minute, Chris sat as still as a statue. At last, his lips formed a soft smile. "I get it," he said softly. "Truly. I do. When Connie died, whatever plans she and I had, those died, too. Some folks—Connie's parents, in particular— think I ought to dedicate the rest of my life to my late wife's memory. But that ain't gonna work. Connie, she left me with a little girl to raise. For Hope's sake, I can't spend the rest of my life mourning her loss. I have to look forward to the future. Hope deserves that."

"You do, too," Reggie whispered.

"We all do," Chris said, his voice firm. His big hand cupped hers. "My timing might not be the best, and I'm probably rushing things, but there's something I've been wanting to tell you for quite a while now."

Reggie tilted her head. Her own moral compass refused to let her pursue a new relationship until she'd stamped "Over and Done" on the previous one. Now that her divorce was official, there were a few things she wanted to say to Chris as well.

The tall man inhaled deeply. "I'm hoping

you'll be a part of my future. Of mine…and Hope's, that is. I'm not saying tomorrow or even next week, but maybe someday?"

Warmth spread through Reggie's chest. She'd been counting the days until she was free to explore how she felt about Chris, to determine if their feelings for one another went deeper than physical attraction. But ten days had passed since her divorce had been finalized, and she was just now learning about it. In her mind, that meant she and Chris had some time to make up.

"How about celebrating my divorce by letting me take you and Hope to Maggie's Diner for dessert tonight?" She knew from previous visits that Hope loved Maggie's custard pudding. As for Chris, he was partial to the diner's apple pie and, well, she was partial to Chris.

"Hope would like that." Chris removed the ball cap that featured the logo of the local hardware store. He twirled it on the tip of one finger. "I'd like it, too."

Reggie smiled. Her love for Sam had died, but her dreams for the future lived on. Oh, she still wanted the home, the family, the promise of forever—that part of her hadn't changed. She suspected that together, she and Chris might make those dreams come true. For now, though, she wanted to take things one step at a time.

Beginning with a family outing at the only other restaurant in Sugar Sand Beach.

Which, she was pretty sure, was the way Chris wanted it, too. With Hope's future at stake, neither of them was going to rush headlong into a relationship.

"Hold still, little bit." Reggie laughed as she tried to zipper the jacket of a squirming Hope. After near-perfect weather during the day, temperatures had fallen into the low fifties as the sun began to sink. Toss in a strong breeze blowing off the ocean, and they all needed to bundle up against the cold for their trip to Maggie's Diner.

"She's quite the wiggle-worm, isn't she?" Erin asked.

"Now that she's walking, she wants to be on the go all the time." Reggie pulled the zipper up to Hope's chin. She should know. Chasing after the toddler in the main house this afternoon had been a big challenge. There were just too many pretty breakables within reach of a curious little girl. Reggie added "childproof the apartment" to her to-do list so that, on those occasions when

Chris and Hope came to visit, they wouldn't have to be on guard the whole time.

She glanced at Erin. "Are you sure you and Ron won't join us for dessert? You're always welcome."

"No, thanks. The latest Maggie Miller book came out yesterday. I'm going to get lost in Blackbird Beach." Erin lifted her iPad. "Besides, Ron's not even here—he's meeting with Nellie to look at a house. It's way over in Panama City, but that's about the closest thing we've been able to find."

Reggie turned away so Erin wouldn't see her smile. So far, Michelle's plan to keep Erin and Ron from signing a lease was working. It helped that Nellie was in on the pact, along with most of the property owners within the Sugar Sand Beach town limits. Now, with less than two weeks to go before the wedding, they only needed to keep their big surprise under wraps for a little while longer.

She pulled up the hood of Hope's jacket. "There. Finally." she sighed. Her success didn't last long. No sooner had she tucked Hope's blond curls beneath the fur-trimmed hood than the baby pushed it off again.

"Oh, you!" Reggie grinned at the little girl. "Daddy's going to want you to wear that till we get in the truck." She repeated the process of covering the child's head.

"Da-da?" Hope's little face crumpled. Her head swung. "Da-da!" she called, louder this time and clearly unhappy that Chris wasn't in the room.

"Want to go see Daddy?" Reggie scooped the baby into her arms and settled her on one hip. "Oomph. You're getting to be a big girl. What's that?" She pretended to listen. "I think Daddy's truck is pulling up right now."

Headlights flashed in the front windows. A rumbling engine settled into a throaty purr. Hope's little body stretched toward the door. "Da-da!" she repeated.

Reggie hoisted the diaper bag over her shoulder. "Tell Nina thanks again for supper. Hope loved the french fries." While the baby thoroughly enjoyed dipping the shoestring potatoes into ketchup, she and Chris and her friends had eaten a simple meal of meatloaf and baked yams.

"She already went upstairs. She said she and Mr. Pibbs were going to relax in front of the TV tonight." Erin slipped her arms into the jacket she took from a nearby coat tree. "I'll walk out with you." She held the door open.

Expecting to see Chris's truck idling at the steps, Reggie stepped onto the porch. Instead,

Chris was helping a fit, gray-haired man pull luggage from the trunk of a sedan. Reggie's brows slammed together. She turned to Erin. "Is that…?"

"Dad? Dad!" Erin asked and answered the question. Darting ahead of Reggie, she raced down the steps.

Careful not to lose her grip on the precious cargo she carried, Reggie followed right behind her sister. "Dad, what are you doing here? I thought you and Mom said you couldn't make it. Where's Mom?"

"My girls!" In a flash, her father's sinewy arms wrapped them both in a hug. "Winnie," he called over one shoulder. "Come on out. Erin and Reggie are here." He stared at the baby on Reggie's hip. "And wait till you see what Reggie has!"

Reggie laughed. "No, Dad. She's not mine. This little one is Chris's little girl." She brushed her fingers under Hope's chin. "You remember me telling you about her, don't you?" She'd recounted several of the toddler's escapades during their weekly phone calls.

Hope, who'd taken one look at the stranger and buried her head in Reggie's shoulder, stirred. "Da-da," she whispered. She held her arms out to Chris, who took the baby.

The car's passenger door shut, and Reggie's mom rushed around the bumper.

"Erin! Reggie!" She grabbed first one daughter and then the next.

Reggie sank into her mother's arms. The floral scent of her mom's favorite perfume wrapped around her, reminding her of home. As far as she could tell, Edwina Bradshaw—Winnie only to her husband—hadn't changed a bit in the nine months since Reggie's last visit to West Virginia. Neither had her dad, for that matter.

At last, her mother held her at arm's length. "You both look wonderful," she said, glancing at Erin. "I can't tell you how glad I am to finally be here. We've been driving for what felt like days."

"It was days, Winnie," said Frank Bradshaw. "Took us three full days on the road to make it all the way down here. Course we spent the night in hotels," he explained, his focus shifting to the other man in the group. "Neither Winnie or I drive much at night anymore. Not if we can help it."

"Did you come across on I-10, sir?" Chris asked politely.

"Nah. We took I-70 out of Wheeling. Eventually hooked up with I-65 and followed that south. We were good till we hit Birmingham. From there, things got a bit complicated.

Missed a turn or two and had to double back. Let me get these bags and maybe someone can tell us where we're gonna sleep." He cast an expectant look at Erin, who held up her hands.

"Don't ask me. Did Michelle know you were coming?"

"Oh, we didn't tell a soul, honey," their mother answered. "Couldn't risk spoiling the surprise."

"Well, it's certainly a surprise. A good one," Erin said, leaning in for another hug.

"This place looks even nicer than it does in the pictures you sent." Frank kicked the bottom step like he was kicking the tire on a car. "Solid, too."

The simple words were high praise coming from her dad, who'd taken up woodworking when he retired. Reggie beamed. Replacing the front steps had been one of the first projects Chris had undertaken when Michelle inherited the property. "Let me take Hope so you can help my dad with the bags," she offered.

Without hesitation, the little girl poured herself into Reggie's waiting arms.

"Well, now. Isn't that nice." Edwina smiled broadly and turned to Erin while the two men pulled several more bags from the trunk. "All right. Let me see this ring I've heard so little about."

Dutifully, Erin stretched out her left hand. Edwina peered down. "Oh, this is gorgeous. Just beautiful!" she gushed.

"Thanks, Mom. It's a keeper." Erin paused before adding, "Ron is, too."

Edwina pursed her lips. "Your father and I always did like that young man. We hated to see the two of you break up. It'll be good to have him back in the family again."

Reggie swore she felt the tension melt off her sister's shoulders as Edwina spoke for both of their parents. The day their mom and dad told them they couldn't make it to the wedding, she and Erin had talked long into the night. Her sister hadn't accepted their parents' feigned excuse of a long-awaited doctor's appointment as a good enough reason to miss her wedding. Nor had she looked forward to trying to convince them that both she and Ron had changed and belonged together.

"And where is Ron?" Their mom looked around as if she expected him to materialize out of thin air.

"He's house-hunting." Erin scuffed one foot through the grass. "We'll need a place to stay while our own house is being built."

"Why?" Their mother's brows drew together. "Can't you stay here?"

"So, Mom, how long can you stay?" Reggie asked in a not too subtle attempt to steer the conversation away from Erin and Ron's living arrangements.

"Why, until the wedding, of course," Edwina responded. Her lips thinned, and she rounded on Reggie. "And before you ask, our feelings for Sam are completely different. Your father never had much use for the likes of him." Her hand fell to her side. Her voice dropping to a whisper, she added, "We *don't* want him back in the family."

"Neither do I, Mom," Reggie said, nodding. "Neither do I." She hugged Hope closer to her chest. "Let's go inside. Chris and I were on our way to the diner in town for dessert. Maybe once you're settled, you can join us?"

"I'll drive," Erin volunteered.

"Why, that sounds perfectly lovely," Edwina agreed as Chris lugged all but the smallest of the suitcases up the steps and into the house. "I can't wait to hear all the wedding plans."

Their father picked up the remaining bag and followed behind.

Laughing and talking, they made it as far as the entryway, where their noisy arrival drew Michelle out of the office at the back of the house. The slim brunette hurried into the room. A round of hugs and surprised greetings followed before Reggie announced, "They're here for the wedding. Where do we want to put them?"

Fortunately, three months as the inn's official hostess had only strengthened Michelle's ability to roll with the punches. Smiling, she turned to Frank and Edwina. "I can offer you two choices. The Trout Suite is on the ground floor and quite convenient. However, we're remodeling the turret over the holidays, and that suite backs up to it. I'm afraid it'll be a bit noisy. Or you can have the Manatee Suite. It's right at the top of the stairs on the second floor and has its own private bath and sitting room." She looked expectantly at Edwina.

"Frank and I don't mind stairs at all, do we, Frank?" She glanced at her husband of forty-five years, who shook his head. "Our house in West Virginia has three flights. We're used to going up and down."

"The Manatee Suite it is, then." Michelle turned to lead them to their little home away from home.

"Mom, Dad?" Reggie kissed them both on their cheeks. "I'm so glad you're here. We'll see you in just a bit at the diner?"

"Of course, honey," her father answered. "We wouldn't miss the chance to spend time with our girls." He inclined his head toward Chris. "And their friends."

Still holding Hope, Reggie started for Chris's truck. She'd get the baby buckled in so that, by the time Chris finished carrying her parents' luggage upstairs, they'd be ready to head for the diner. She smiled. This morning had seen the end of one dream and what might just be the beginning of a new one. This afternoon, she'd had the chance to play with Hope, something that always lifted her spirits. Now, with a surprise visit from her parents, a day that had gotten off to a miserable start was ending on a high note.

Four

Nina

A fternoon, Chef." In the hallway that led from the back of the living room to the turret, Zeke's second in command touched the brim of his baseball hat.

"Hey, Toby. Zeke still inside?" Nina edged closer to the wall to let the men leaving on their lunch break pass.

"Yes, ma'am," Toby said, already moving farther down the hall.

Behind him, the newest member of Zeke's crew made a show of ogling more than the picnic basket Nina carried. "Mmm-mm. Somethin's sure lookin' good. What's cookin'?"

Nina gave the young man the same amount of attention she'd given the construction workers who'd whistled and jeered as she passed by a work site on the big city streets—absolutely none. As she continued on down the hall, she heard one set of footsteps slow.

"Didn't your mama raise you better 'n that? Show some respect! You want some young buck makin' a pass at your sister?" hissed Toby.

"Sorry, man," came a somewhat embarrassed response. "Won't happen again."

"It better not," the older man said pointedly. "Chef Nina is the boss's girl. You mess with her, you're gonna get yourself fired."

Nina smiled as she moved out of earshot. She had no doubt whatsoever that she could put the youngster in his place in a heartbeat, but she couldn't deny that it felt nice knowing Toby had her back. She tried the term "the boss's girl" on for size and decided she liked it.

At the entrance to the turret, she opened the door that Zeke insisted remain closed in order to minimize the spread of dust and dirt through the rest of the house. Inside, opaque plastic formed another barrier against the grime. Nina pushed aside one of the thick sheets that hung from sturdy wires. Exposed wooden slats and two-by-fours circled the unfinished wood floor. She craned her neck and stared up at the domed ceiling more than two floors above. The round turret stirred a memory from her favorite movie.

In it, the hero had hidden in a grain silo and had nearly been buried in an avalanche of corn.

She shivered and checked the skylight. No corn.

On the other side of the room, Zeke stood with his back to her. He walked along one section of the exposed framing. As he moved back and forth, he tapped the wall with the handle of a large screwdriver.

Nina watched with interest. Two years ago, her landlord had discovered termites in the apartment next to hers. A pest control company had been called in to do a thorough inspection before the entire building had been tented and treated to a noxious mix of poisonous gases. The man who did the job had tapped and knocked on every wooden surface, just like Zeke was doing now.

"Whatcha doing?" she called. Her voice echoed in the empty room. She crossed her fingers. Please don't let it be termites, she prayed.

"Tryin' to figure out what's wrong with this wall. It's off a might." Zeke's deep voice bounced off the bare wood behind her.

"Rotten?" Nina asked. She set the heavy picnic basket on a makeshift table made of plyboard and sawhorses.

"Nah. The measurements don't feel right." Zeke pointed. "I'm pretty sure this here is a false wall." He rapped on it with the screwdriver. "When I compare the turret to the living room and the hall, it seems like this ought to be another five or six feet back."

Nina frowned. Slowly, she let her gaze travel around the space. Nothing in the room had been painted in the hundred years the house had been standing. If there was a hidden compartment in the area Zeke indicated, someone had done a remarkable job of making it blend in with the rest of the slats and studs. Okay, maybe the section Zeke had pointed out was a slightly lighter shade of brown, but that was the only difference she could spot. Not that it mattered. Zeke had been in construction his entire life. If he said the measurements were off, they were off.

But why?

"Do you think there's a body hidden in there?" She shivered again, this time for an entirely different reason.

Zeke laughed out loud. "You've been watching too much of those murder mysteries you like so much. I can think of a dozen reasons someone would erect a false wall. None of them involve murder."

Nina's hands shook slightly. "Name one."

"Okay," he said slowly. "How about this—at some point, Ms. Simmons or her parents might have wanted to turn this room into an art studio. You know, to paint watercolors or such."

Nina glanced up at the two small windows on the northern side of the house. She shook her head. "This space has terrible lighting. The sun porch would be a much better place for an easel."

Zeke shrugged. "Maybe someone took up weaving and wanted a place for a loom. Or maybe Nancy's parents planned on having another baby and wanted to turn this area into a nursery."

"I can go along with a weaving room," Nina said. Working with textiles had never been her thing, but the pastry chef at Cafe Chez Jacques had quilted in her spare time. "That still doesn't explain why they'd wall off a section."

"Aesthetics, maybe?" Zeke's voice hiked at the end, turning the statement into a question. "They may just have wanted a circular room, and a niche jutting out of it ruined the look. We may never know why, but I can for sure find out if I'm right."

"What are you going to do?"

"This afternoon, I'm going to take a sledge-hammer and knock a hole in the wall. Right about…here." He slid his hands back and forth over a spot. "If I'm right, we'll prove this was a false wall after all. Might even find something interesting behind it."

Nina swallowed. Whatever he found, if he found anything at all, it probably wouldn't be good. Then there was the damage he'd cause. The turret backed up to the living room. She hated to think what Zeke's sledgehammer would do to the hundred-year-old plaster walls. "And if you're wrong?" she asked quietly.

Zeke scuffed a booted foot along the floorboards. "If I'm wrong, I'll bust right through and make a bunch of work for myself. But at least I'll know for sure. If there's mold or something behind here, we need to fix it now rather than later." He must have noticed the basket perched between the sawhorses because his dark eyes brightened. "You brought lunch?"

"Yeah. I thought we could have a picnic. Of sorts." She patted the blanket that hung over one of her arms.

"Aw, you didn't have to do that. I don't mind comin' to the cafe." Zeke slipped his screwdriver into his tool belt and dusted his hands.

"I'm usually so busy there we don't get a chance to say more than a few words to each other. Here, I thought, we'd get to spend the better part of an hour together." She tilted her head at a saucy angle. "Alone," she added.

"Who needs food when we have each other?" Zeke crossed the room in three long strides. Something that looked an awful lot like desire flickered in his eyes. Arms thick as tree trunks drew her into a warm embrace, and he brushed kisses through her hair.

Nina let the blanket fall to the floor. Folding herself into Zeke, she inhaled the heady blend of sawdust and sweat mixed with the faint smell of his aftershave and a scent that was his alone. She tipped her head to his and was rewarded when their lips met. Before things heated up too much, though, they both drew apart.

"You know I'd like nothing more than for us to put that blanket to good use," Zeke rasped. "But there ain't no lock on that door, and the guys walk in and out of here all the time."

Nina inhaled another deep breath before she stepped out of Zeke's arms. "One day," she promised. "Today, though, let's do lunch." She smiled. "I hope you're hungry 'cause I brought lots." Picking up the blanket, she shook it out and spread it over a relatively clean spot on the floor.

Zeke laughed, a hearty sound that made Nina's heart beat a little faster. "I can always eat."

"Good. I need your opinion on something."

"Oh, yeah? If it's food, I'm your man." Taking the basket from the makeshift table, he set it gently on the blanket. His legs folded beneath him as he lowered himself to the floor.

"I'm testing some of the recipes for Christmas dinner, and I want your take on them." Ordinarily, she didn't rely on second opinions. But this was the most important meal she'd ever prepared. Because not only would the people she loved be gathered around the table, but it was also Erin and Ron's wedding feast. For such a momentous occasion, every dish had to be absolutely perfect.

Nina didn't have any questions about the entrées. Her standing rib roast was sheer, mouthwatering perfection and a favorite of Erin's. A rich seafood lasagna filled with scallops and fresh crab, plump shrimp and chunks of whitefish would exceed all Ron's expectations. But the side dishes? No, she wasn't nearly as certain about those. Candied carrots or yams? Crisp Brussels sprouts drizzled with a balsamic reduction or that tried-and-true favorite, creamed spinach? Baked or scalloped potatoes? Or should she skip the potatoes altogether and go with a nice rice pilaf?

She opened the lid of the picnic basket.

Inside, a dozen containers held freshly prepared samples of her favorite contenders for spots on the table.

Zeke stole a peck on her cheek as he gazed at the wealth of choices. "You don't expect me to eat all that, do you? I'll get fat." He patted his flat stomach.

"No, silly." She aimed a goofy smile at the big man who'd won her heart. "I just want you to try a little bit of this. A little bit of that. Like you'd do if you went to the caterer for a tasting."

"Oh, yeah?" Zeke's heavy brows lifted. "Can't say as I've ever been to one of those, but I've seen 'em on TV. I'm game. Want some help?"

"Sure." Nina took the first couple of containers from the basket. "So you and Donna didn't have a big wedding?" she asked as Zeke added a couple more plastic tubs to the row she'd started.

"Nope. Her parents insisted on holding the reception in the church hall. Just fruit punch and cake. No dinner. Definitely no dancing. I kinda wished we'd had that part."

Nina tilted her head. "I'll let you take me dancing sometime." She added a final container to the neat row.

"That's a date." Zeke unfolded his long legs. With his legs outstretched, he leaned back on his arms. "Now about that lunch—bring it on!" he said while anticipation glowed in his expression.

Nina pried the lids off several of the tubs. Immediately, a heady mix of appetizing scents filled the air. While she spooned bite-size portions onto paper plates, she asked Zeke about his plans for the room.

"We're adding a second level," he explained. "The living area and an efficiency kitchen will be down here. Michelle picked out one of those combo stove-oven-microwave units and a refrigerator. There won't be much counter space, so I'm going to build a small island that will serve three functions. First, it'll separate the kitchen from the rest of the apartment. It'll also provide more storage and counter space. Finally, they'll be able to eat at it, so they won't need a table and chairs. It'll go over there." He pointed to the wall that abutted the rest of the house.

"That sounds great," she said, handing him a plate and a fork. She'd seen the plans, but she hadn't been able to visualize them until Zeke and his crew had emptied the turret, an area that had been used primarily for storage. "What'd you do with all the stuff you found in here?"

"Whatever was worth keeping, we toted up to the attic. The rest, we put in the trash."

She nodded. That explained the rickety

bookcase and the two chairs with busted seats she'd spotted in the trash pile.

Zeke chewed thoughtfully on a Brussels sprout. "You know, I don't usually like these"— he tapped one of the round green halves with his fork—"but this isn't half-bad."

"Do you like it better than the spinach?" Nina asked.

"Oh, definitely." He gave an exaggerated shudder. "Spinach, yuck." He pushed the offensive sample to one side and speared a carrot. Waving it to the right of the kitchen area, he said, "There'll be a full bath right over there. The rest of this space will be one large living area. We'll put the bedroom and another full bath in the loft." He chewed on his lower lip.

Nina recognized that look. Zeke wore it whenever something weighed heavily on his mind. "What? You don't like the carrots either?"

"No, they're very good. I'll take some more if there's any left." He held out his plate. While she gave him the rest of the vegetable that had been butter-roasted to a crisp and then drizzled with honey, he said, "What's bothering me is the staircase. Michelle wanted it along that side of the house." He pointed to the spot where he planned to put the kitchen. "But in order keep the costs down to a reasonable amount, we need to tie into the existing plumbing. The pipes are all on that side. That's where the kitchen and baths have to go."

Following his logic, Nina nodded. She nibbled on one of the tasty carrots from her own plate. Those were definitely going on the menu for the wedding dinner, she decided. "Can you put the staircase over there?" She gestured to the wall opposite the kitchen area.

"No." Zeke's dark hair shifted. He pointed to the two windows on the outside wall. "The stairs would block the only natural light coming into the room. I don't want to do that." He scooped up a bite of the yams. "Hey, do I taste orange? And what's that? Tarragon?"

"Yep." She was quite proud of the recipe she'd concocted for the yams. Most cooks used maple syrup for the glaze, but the tangy orange enhanced, rather than smothered, the sweetness of the root vegetable. Meanwhile, the tarragon provided a nice back note.

"I think this is my favorite so far." Zeke chewed for a moment and swallowed. "Yeah, those are good. You need those."

Two orange vegetables at the same table? Nina shrugged. Better than an all-green meal or, worse, an all-white one. "So where are you going to put the staircase?" she asked.

"I don't have much choice. I'll have to build it in the middle of the room. I don't much like it there, though. Makes it the first thing you see when you walk into the suite. Plus, it'll take up a lot of valuable floor space. Right now, with nothing in here, this place looks plenty big for two people. Once we start hauling in couches and chairs, though, things'll get tight in a hurry. That'd be okay for guests who were staying a week or two, but Ron and Erin will live here for the better part of a year."

"Hmmm." Nina tapped her chin. Room design wasn't her forte, but she saw Zeke's point. She slid her fingers along his forearm. "You'll find a solution. I know you will." Zeke had a solid reputation for satisfying his customers. She had no doubt he'd mull the problem over until he found the perfect answer. She checked her watch. None of his crew had disturbed their lunch hour, but they'd be trooping back to work soon.

"So, what'd you think?" she asked, sweeping her hand over the tubs. Most were empty. Only the creamed spinach remained virtually untouched. "Besides the carrots and the yams, are there any keepers?"

"The Brussels sprouts, for sure. And I liked those little—what'd you call 'em, the things with the mushrooms."

"The pinwheels?" Caramelized mushrooms filled the tightly rolled puff pastry. She hadn't thought he'd like them. She glanced at the empty container. I guess he did, she thought.

"Yeah, those were pretty good. The scalloped potatoes are sure to be a hit." He closed another of the containers with a snap. "Can I, uh, ask for one more thing?"

"Sure." There was little she'd deny him—he knew that, didn't he?

"Green beans," he said with a certain finality. "Nothing fancy. Just plain, cooked green beans. Lily will try just about anything, but Megs is a bit fussy. That girl never saw a green bean she didn't like, though."

The simple request touched Nina's heart. Zeke was such a good dad. Despite the hours it took away from his day job, he attended every one of his daughters' school and sports activities. His weekends and holidays revolved around their schedules. And he did his absolute best to make the most of the time they spent together. How could she turn down such a sweet request?

"You got it. Green beans it is," she promised. She began gathering up their plates and utensils. "I'm glad Megan and Lily are coming to the wedding."

"Yeah, me, too," Zeke said as he loaded the

now empty containers into the picnic basket. "I wasn't sure Donna would give them up on Christmas Day." According to their court-arranged visitation schedule, Zeke's daughters alternated spending Christmas and Thanksgiving with their parents. This year, it was their mother's turn to have the girls for the final holiday of the year. "But she appreciates how much time you spend with them, especially Lily. And she knows what a good influence Erin's had on Megan—taking her kayaking and fishing like she does. Megs used to be pretty sullen. Her attitude's improved a lot over the last few months."

Nina's eyes moistened. Lily dreamed of becoming a chef someday. Though Nina recognized that the preteen's goals might change several times in the coming years, she enjoyed helping the little girl develop basic cooking skills. As for Megan, the teenager greatly preferred the outdoors, but whenever she joined them in the kitchen, Megs was always a delight. She brushed her eyes. "Please give Donna our thanks—mine and Erin's. It means a lot to have both your daughters at the wedding."

"Will do. Donna took 'em shopping for new dresses and shoes." He stretched. "I'm picking them up at two on Christmas afternoon. We'll be here in plenty of time for the ceremony and dinner."

The rumbling sound of a big engine seeped through the walls.

"That's probably Toby and the guys back from lunch," Zeke said. "He must'a taken the whole crew to Maggie's today." Outside, doors slammed and a man laughed. "They'll be here in a minute. But before they get here…" Tracing one finger along Nina's jaw line, he murmured, "Thanks for lunch."

Aware that Zeke's crew could walk through the door any minute, they kept the kiss short and sweet. When it was over, he stood and helped her to her feet. Nina quickly folded the blanket. By the time she'd finished, the workers had arrived. As they fanned out and began tackling their assigned tasks, Nina said, "I'd like to be here when you open up that wall. If you don't mind."

"No problem. I'll send someone to get you when I'm ready. Won't be till later this afternoon or first thing tomorrow. I want to take a few more measurements just to be sure."

She smiled. "I'll be in the kitchen when you want me."

"I always want you."

Zeke's deep voice whispered in her ear. The seductive grin he added left no doubt to his meaning, and Nina felt her face—and her insides—heat in response. Someday, she vowed as she headed for the exit. Someday soon, she was going to take a certain sexy man up on his offer and see where it led them.

Five

Michelle

Her breath caught in her throat. The 9-1-1 text demanding she and Reggie join Nina in the turret sent fear rippling through Michelle's belly. Had one of the workmen been hurt? Did she need to call an ambulance?

"No, no, no, no, no," she murmured, her feet already in motion.

Memories of the day she'd found Allen facedown on the carpet by his desk, the phone still clutched in his hand, bubbled to the surface. To this day, she still had no idea who had been on the other end of the line. She'd grabbed her husband's cell and simply hit the End Call button. She supposed she'd punched in the emergency number next. She remembered suddenly being surrounded by men and women who wore solemn faces above black uniforms. Someone had ushered her out of the office, but to be honest, the next several hours were hazy, as if she'd dreamed them or they'd happened to someone else. Her next clear recollection was of Reggie and Nina sitting beside her as she placed the most difficult phone calls of her life.

A tremor shook her. A rushing noise filled her ears. The world grayed around the edges.

"Stop," she told herself. She found the nearest wall and leaned against it while she fought for control. For a long minute, she concentrated on breathing like they'd taught her in the grief support group.

In and out. Nice and easy.

The panic slowly retreated like an outgoing tide. Her thoughts cleared.

If someone needed medical attention, Nina had already called for an ambulance. There was nothing for her to do.

If it were a true emergency, Nina would have included Erin in the text. But she hadn't. So whatever the problem was, it probably didn't involve life or limb.

She took in a cleansing breath and emptied her lungs. After pushing herself off the wall, she continued on toward the turret at a pace slightly less than her previous mad dash.

Reggie, still going full tilt, caught up with her before she reached the living room. "What's wrong?" the younger woman asked as her footsteps matched Michelle's stride for stride. Reggie's sun-darkened complexion had paled until her freckles stood out on her cheeks like brown smudges.

"I don't know. I got the same text you did." Michelle saw her own panic reflected in the depths of her friend's blue eyes.

"I hope everyone is okay."

"Me, too," Michelle whispered as they hurried down the short hall to the door that opened into the construction area.

Once beyond the protective sheeting, she had no trouble locating the source of the problem. Zeke's crew clustered in one spot. As Michelle and Reggie approached the group, the men parted to make a path for them. Zeke and Nina stood up front, where they peered through a large opening in the wooden slats. The contractor played a flashlight over the jagged edges of the hole. A lethal-looking sledgehammer leaned against a nearby stud.

Had Zeke punched through the wall on purpose? Why on earth would he do such a thing?

Michelle cleared her throat. "Zeke? Nina? What's going on?"

Nina spun toward her. "You'll never guess what we found!"

Reggie sighed audibly. Her shoulders slumped. "No one's hurt?" she asked. Her voice shook.

Nina's eyes widened as her gaze bounced between Reggie and Michelle. "Oh, geez." Her hand flew to her mouth. "I'm sorry. I'm so sorry. I didn't think… I never considered…" Her voice trailed off.

"So," Michelle said, just to be clear, "no one is hurt. We aren't expecting an ambulance. Or sirens?"

"No. Nothing like that. I swear." Nina peeled her hand off her mouth and raised it as if she was saying a pledge.

"Okay." Michelle forcefully exhaled. Relief so real it left her giddy coursed through her. The next time the four of them got together, they'd talk about the proper—or improper—use of a 9-1-1 text. Now, though, was not the time or the place. Not with Zeke and his entire work crew listening in on the conversation. She mustered a smile and was surprised when it didn't wobble. "In that case, what's so important that we had to drop everything and rush here?"

Michelle felt Nina's hand grasp hers and give it a tight squeeze. The chef repeated the motion with Reggie before pulling both of them forward.

"You have to see this to believe it."

Following Nina's lead, Michelle stepped closer to the wall. With Reggie at her side, she glanced into a jagged hole that someone—presumably Zeke—had created. After a few inches, the light faded into an impenetrable darkness. She shook her head. "I can't see a thing."

"Me, either," Reggie added.

"Sorry. Here. Use this." Zeke handed Reggie a heavy flashlight.

With it resting on the bottom of the opening, the younger woman played a strong beam of light over what appeared to be a small chamber. Michelle caught a quick glimpse of a bicycle, a pair of skis, a ball and a tennis racket before her gaze landed on a spiral staircase.

She turned to Reggie. "How high up does that go?"

Reggie tried several different angles, but the light faded after ten feet or so, and the steps disappeared.

"Someone built this false wall long after the house was completed." Zeke rapped his knuckles on a section of the lath. "It's about six feet across and, from what we can tell, it goes all the way up to the top of the turret, same as the rest of the walls. Stands to reason the staircase goes that high, too. Or at least as far as the attic."

Michelle blinked. Well, this was a surprise. Stepping away from the opening, she peered up at the tall man beside her. "Does the attic have access to the staircase?" She herself had never explored the nooks and crannies of the largely unused space. If she had her way, she never would. Dust bunnies and spiders ruled that domain. As far as she was concerned, they were welcome to it.

"I'll take a look this afternoon," Zeke promised. "I want to check out the second floor, too. It's possible there was a landing up there at one time."

"Why would anyone wall off a staircase?" Reggie mused. "And what's with all the bikes and stuff?"

"I don't know, but I think we have to find out." Michelle took a second look at the items that had been piled around the foot of the stairs. Without actually handling them and gauging their flex, it was hard to tell if the vintage skis had been made for a woman or a man, but the two-wheeler was definitely a girl's bike. She blinked away a sudden dampness. She had a pretty good idea about who had once owned the equipment and why it had been tucked away out of sight and out of mind, but she didn't want to say anything until they learned what else had been hidden behind the wall. She looked at Zeke. "Were you planning to open it all up?"

"Yeah, I reckon. Unless you tell me otherwise. At first, I was worried someone built this to hide mold or some kinda rot. Doesn't look like that's the case, though." Taking the flashlight, he slowly worked it over the original wall, one that backed up to the living room. "I can't spot any water damage. No mildew. No black fuzz. Course, we'll give it a thorough going over."

"The good news is, if the staircase is sturdy enough, Zeke won't have to build another one," Nina pointed out.

Michelle canted her head. "Is that true?"

"Maybe. That's all I can say till we take out the entire wall, but from the little I can see, there's no sign of rust or loose steps." Zeke grasped a loose piece of lath in one of his large hands and pulled it. The thin wood slats splintered and fell to the floor. "If the rest of the staircase is in as good a shape as the bottom, it's quite a find." He pointed. "Look at the details. This is rightly called a spindle staircase. Some-body spent some serious money on it."

"Taking all this down, though"—Michelle eyed the wall that stretched to the top of the house—"that's not going to be cheap."

"No, but neither is building a staircase. Even the simple wooden one I was planning on for the loft. It's possible the costs will offset one another."

Whether they did or not, she and Nina and Reggie couldn't ask Zeke to simply patch over the hole and move on. Like the builder said, whatever was back there, they needed to know about it. She glanced at Reggie and Nina for confirmation and saw agreement in their eyes.

"Okay. Go ahead and knock down the false wall." As he started to move away, Michelle plucked at the big man's upper arm. "But Zeke?"

"Yep." He turned questioning eyes on her.

"Please save everything in there." She hooked a thumb at the chamber. If she was right about their origins, the items in the closet were a part of her history.

"You got it. Where would you like me to move it?"

"Into the office off the kitchen for now." She'd take her time sorting through everything once it was in a more accessible location. And who knew? Maybe the items that had been hidden away for decades would shed a little more light on her birth mother.

"Has anyone seen Erin?" Two days after the discovery of the hidden staircase, Michelle stepped into the kitchen. She normally steered clear of the chef's domain when the cafe was open, but she was on her way to her office, and the quickest path led right past Nina's prep station.

"She and Ron went to Polly's Posies to finalize their floral arrangements for the wedding." Looking both at ease and in charge in her chef's whites, Nina studied a chicken and pesto sandwich on the counter. She straightened a lettuce leaf before reaching for a squeeze bottle filled with something orange. Tipping the bottle, she drew a circle of sauce around the plated sandwich.

"So they aren't here." Relief softened Michelle's shoulders as she took another step toward the door that led to the back office. Passing in front of Nina, she caught a whiff of a spicy scent as her friend returned the bottle to its holder.

The chef slid the finished plate onto a nearby rack. From there, Gwen would take the order to

Table Five when the waitress made her next trip through the kitchen. Nina caught Michelle's eye. "Did you need her for something? Anything I can help you with?"

"No." Michelle paused at the counter that served as Nina's station. Not wanting Ethan or Viola to overhear, she lowered her voice. "The linens for their apartment came yesterday. I want to make sure we have everything we need so that, as soon as Zeke and his crew finish painting, I can get in there and decorate."

"I can't believe the wedding is only a week away." Nina likewise spoke softly while she added the finishing touches to the next dish. This one held a scrumptious-looking BLT and a pile of glistening french fries. She filled a paper cup with tomato chutney and tucked it between the sandwich and the fries before adding the plate to the others on the rack.

"A week from tomorrow. I only hope Zeke finishes in time. Have they started on the second floor yet?"

Nina's head bobbed. "They're fast! I took coffee to the crew this morning, and there's scaffolding everywhere. They'd already drywalled everything down to the loft area, and they are laying that flooring today. Now that they don't have to spend time building a staircase, they're actually ahead of schedule."

Michelle expelled a long, thready breath. Zeke and his men had made quick work of dismantling the false wall. Just as the contractor had predicted, the spindle staircase was in near-perfect shape and only needed a fresh coat of black paint to restore it to its former beauty.

"Do you really think Erin and Ron will like what we've done?" she asked.

Nina laughed. "If they don't, they can always find someplace else to live, and we'll redecorate."

"I wish I could be sure about the colors, but we couldn't actually ask them without letting them in on the secret." Michelle's original plan had been to convert the turret into a sumptuous honeymoon suite. However, while lacy window treatments, satin sheets and fluffy bearskin rugs were great for a romantic getaway, they didn't hold up so well in the long run. She couldn't quite picture Erin and Ron being happy with them for the year it would take to build their house. "You don't think they've figured it out, do you?"

Nina shook her head. "Last I heard, they were still determined to find a rental. Nellie promised she'd have something for them by the time they get back from the Keys." She winked.

Thankful they'd included the Realtor in their

conspiracy, Michelle gave a half-smile. "I'll be in the office for a while. Give me a heads-up if they come back before I finish." Her heels tapping against the hardwood floors, she took two steps before turning back to the chef. "I won't be here for supper tonight. Dave has business in town, so he's picking me up after and taking me to Maggie's Diner."

Nina shook her head. "You two are sure seeing a lot of each other."

Michelle's head bobbed up and down. She and her former attorney met for coffee whenever he came to Sugar Sand Beach or she needed something in Destin. They'd fallen into the habit of having dinner together every Friday night. It was one habit Michelle didn't want to break.

At the door to the office, she pulled a set of house keys from the pocket of a pair of slim-fitting jeans. Several weeks earlier, she'd declared the space off-limits to Erin by citing 'wedding secrets.' But once packages containing everything the newlyweds would need to set up housekeeping began to arrive, she'd taken the added measure of locking the door. Now that Nancy Simmons's belongings filled one corner of the room, it was even more important that Erin didn't walk in unannounced.

Michelle had wracked her brain for some way

to explain the discovery of Nancy's old bike and skis and had come up empty-handed. How could she tell Erin about them without mentioning the hidden wall or the staircase? And if she mentioned those, Erin would figure out what was really going on in the turret, wouldn't she?

Michelle shook her head. She'd say one thing about Erin—the blonde was one smart cookie. As a woman who'd spent twenty years traveling the globe on her own, she wouldn't have survived otherwise. Michelle had no doubt that one glimpse of the construction area, the piles of throw pillows and linens stacked in the office, or Nancy's belongings, and her friend would put it all together. So, yeah. The office door would remain locked for now.

Michelle gave the equipment neatly stacked in one corner of the room a glance and smiled. Her birth mother had grown up in a different era, one in which handwritten notes were the preferred method of communication. The letter Nancy had placed in Dave's safekeeping had been proof of that. The moment Michelle had peered through the hole in the false wall and spotted Nancy's bike, she'd wondered if her birth mother might have left another missive behind. Sure enough, tucked inside the bike's wicker basket had been a note. Tomorrow, while

Erin was off on her morning run, Michelle planned to share what she'd learned with Nina and Reggie.

But for now, she had work to do and a schedule to keep. It began with the boxes she'd stacked in the closet. She'd had great fun mixing and matching items from several sources, but now came the moment of truth. Were the color charts on the various websites accurate? Was the pale yellow one vendor called "Honey pot" the same as another one's "Lemon Leaf"? According to the swatches and chart numbers they were, but there was always a chance that two stores would have entirely different hues for "Buttercup."

She'd named the rest of the suites in the inn after the fish and mammals commonly found in the area. The Manatee and Dolphin, Mahi and Redfish, Tarpon and Trout suites had all been decorated in keeping with their names. In order to make the apartment stand out, though, she'd chosen Erin's favorite shade of yellow for the walls and accents, with touches of the green Ron often wore for the rest. If it all came together as she hoped it would, the result would be a warm and inviting oasis for the newlyweds. Which, now that she thought about it, was the perfect name for the hideaway.

Grabbing her phone, she composed a text for Reggie. *We're going to call the turret rooms 'The Oasis.' Can you make a sign for it this week?* Using driftwood she'd found on their beach, Reggie had created the pretty signage that hung on the door of each of the other suites.

Love! Reggie texted back right away. *I'm on it.*

Satisfied that the job was in good hands, Michelle took a utility knife from the desk drawer. She slit the tape on the first box and pulled out a large, zippered container. According to the packing list, this was the duvet for the king-size bed that would go in the loft. She unzipped the clear vinyl storage bag and began pulling out the cover. Her fingers sank into the luxurious linen created out of organic flax. Her lips curved into a smile. Erin was going to love this, she thought.

After fluffing the duvet cover, she hung it from an oversize hanger in the closet. Most of the wrinkles would fall out on their own over the next few days. Any that didn't, she'd banish with a garment steamer.

One by one, she opened the rest of the boxes. She closed her eyes for a moment while she imagined the cheery curtains with their yellow and green stripes hanging at the two windows. The colors matched perfectly with the yellow sheets she'd ordered for the bed. She knew little about Ron's sleeping habits, but during her many travels, Erin had spent countless nights under a thin blanket on a cot or in a sleeping bag. Which had given her a deep appreciation for the wonder of good bed linens. The bamboo sheets Michelle had selected came highly recommended and, running her fingers lightly over the silky material, she understood why. Another set in pale green would let the couple mix and match. The towels were thick, fluffy and exactly the right shade. The only disappointments were the potholders and dishrags she'd ordered. Gaudy yellow sunflowers arrayed against an olive-green background gave the them a garish look. She folded those right back into the box they'd come in.

The first of several loads of sheets and towels was in the wash, and she'd broken down all cardboard for recycling when raised voices in the kitchen caught her attention. She froze and listened closely. Had Erin and Ron returned home earlier than expected? It didn't sound like them. She bit her lip as she eyed the office door. Had she locked it after she closed it? Deciding she couldn't risk having the wrong people barge in on her, she quickly crossed the room.

The closer she got to the door, the less the

voices coming from the kitchen sounded like her friends. Leaning forward, she frowned in concentration. Viola spoke loudly, a change for the soft-spoken cook, and a sure sign that something unexpected was underway. She didn't hear Ethan, but then again, the young man only voiced his opinion when someone asked for it. Nina didn't sound at all upset. Excited, maybe, but not distraught, so whatever was happening, it wasn't necessarily a bad thing.

She was about to leave the office and find out what was going on for herself when the last voice in the world she'd expected to hear asked, "Where's Mummy?" and someone else cautioned, "Shhhh. She'll hear you!"

What were Aaron and Ashley doing here?

Michelle shook her head as if to clear it. She had to be mistaken. The twins had chosen to spend the winter break with friends this year. Why, she'd spoken with her daughter only yesterday. Ash had been at her sorority sister's house outside Boston. They'd hit the slopes in the Berkshires for a couple of days, but they planned to spend most of the holidays organizing a program for at-risk girls similar to the one Ashley had been in charge of last summer. As for Aaron, he and another intern at CJX were working on a special project they needed to complete by the first of the year. Their schedule was so tight, they only planned to take a few hours off on Christmas Day.

Someone pounded on the office door before Michelle had time to think things through. Her heart in her throat, she pulled it open…and was immediately swept into her children's waiting arms. Giggling and laughing like, well, like schoolchildren, Ashley and Aaron crowed about pulling one over on their mom while Michelle gave them each teary hugs.

"I can't believe you're here," she exclaimed when she had a chance to catch her breath. "When did you get in? How long can you stay?" Her mind raced with questions. Nina, Ethan and Viola stood nearby, looking exceptionally happy. She gave Nina a pointed glance. "Did you know?"

The chef shook her head. "Nope. They kept it a secret from everyone."

"We wanted it to be a surprise, Mummy," Ashley explained.

"Our Christmas present," Aaron added.

Michelle leaned in for another round of hugs. "I can't think of a better Christmas present than this." She wiped eyes that had instantly filled with tears when she saw her children standing at the door. "Are you hungry? Do you want something to eat? Where are your bags?"

"I could use a glass of sweet tea," Ashley said. "No one makes it as good as Aunt Nina."

"You know me. I'm always hungry." Aaron eyed the tall club sandwich on the serving rack. "That looks good."

"Why don't you three grab a table in the dining room. Gwen will bring you your food and drinks." Although she gave each of the twins an indulgent smile, Nina made shooing motions with her hands.

"Come on." Michelle linked arms with Ashley and Aaron. "Let's get out of here." She had no doubt that Viola, Ethan and Nina had stopped whatever they'd been doing to greet the twins. Although it was the end of the lunch rush, a few customers still waited for their meals.

"So, Mummy." Ashley placed her fingers on Michelle's forearm as the trio headed for a quiet table in the corner of the dining area. "Have you lost weight?"

"A few pounds." Nine to be exact, and dropping them hadn't been easy. Between Nina's calorie-laden cooking and the occasional meal with Dave, the only way she'd been able to burn off the fat had been by adding an extra mile to her morning power walks along the beach. But fitting into her first pair of skinny jeans had made the effort worthwhile.

"You aren't working too hard, are you?" Aaron held out a chair for her.

"Surprisingly, no," Michelle answered as she sat. "Now that we're open for business, the hardest part is behind us. We have a regular cleaning crew. They keep the house spic-and-span. I sweep the porch in the morning because I like to." Even though some of their guests had been early risers, it was rare to find any of them sitting in one of the rattan chairs before sunrise. She loved spending those first few minutes of the day sweeping away the cobwebs—both the literal and figurative ones—that had appeared overnight. "For the most part, though, I spend my days checking inventory, placing orders and paying bills." She made a face.

Gwen slid glasses of sweet iced tea and a basket of piping hot corn fritters on the table. "Compliments of the chef, y'all," said the waitress. She pointed to the round balls with their liberal coating of powdered sugar. "What else can I get ya?"

Michelle smiled up at the woman who managed the dining room with efficiency and flare. "Gwen, these are my children, Aaron and Ashley. They've arrived for a surprise visit and will be staying here through the end of the year." Though the cafe would close for the holiday break after today's shift, she had to share the good news with the waitress.

The usual round of hearty holiday greetings followed. While they munched on corn fritters and, later, Aaron's sandwich and the salads Nina had insisted on sending out for Michelle and Ashley, the twins explained the lengths they'd gone to in order to arrange a trip without their mother finding out about it. They brought her up to speed with what was going on in their lives, providing the kind of detail they hadn't been able to give during weekly phone calls. She filled them in on the goings-on in Sugar Sand Beach, including the Christmas parade the following day. Finally, the twins talked about their vacation plans, which, apparently, involved lots of time soaking up the rays on the beach and hanging out with Dave's daughter Sara.

"Speaking of Dave—" Ashley snagged a french fry from her brother's plate and dunked it in a mound of ketchup. "How are things between you and Destin's favorite attorney?"

Michelle felt her cheeks warm, and she braced herself. Her daughter's behavior this summer had been heartbreaking. She wasn't going to have to endure a repeat of it, was she? Struggling not to overreact, she spoke slowly. "Everything is fine."

"Relax, Mummy." Ashley sipped her tea. "We just want to make sure you're happy."

"She's right, Mom. We all miss Dad." Aaron stared out the window for a long beat. When he spoke again, his voice was strained. "But he'd want you to be happy. If Dave does that for you, then we're glad you're seeing someone."

"Well…" Michelle hesitated. She didn't honestly think the twins would fly all the way to Florida just to pick a fight, did she? And they certainly sounded sincere. She took a breath.

"Dave and I meet for coffee once or twice a week. We have a standing dinner date on Friday nights." She drummed her fingers on the table. The tall attorney had become more than a friend to her—she couldn't deny it. It was time the twins came to grips with the fact that their mother had a life of her own. That one day, she might even get married again. When and if that happened, she expected them to support her decision. Just like she supported theirs. After all, Ashley and Aaron were both adults with lives of their own. They wouldn't tolerate her interference in their relationships. And she wouldn't dream of stepping in, not as long as whoever they dated treated them each with love and respect.

"That's wonderful, Mummy." Ashley leaned in for a hug. "But wait!" A frown formed across the young woman's brow. "This is Friday. Do you have a date tonight?"

"Ordinarily. But I'll cancel it." Much as she didn't want to, she'd have to reschedule her dinner date for another time. She wasn't the kind of mother who abandoned her children—even her grown children—after they'd gone to such lengths to visit her.

"Don't do that," Ashley protested. She and Aaron shared a look. At his nearly imperceptible nod, Ashley asked, "What if we fixed dinner for you here?"

"We'll make that chicken parm dish you like," Aaron said, continuing his sister's thought. "Some baked potatoes."

"I bet we could rustle up some green beans and a big salad," Ashley finished.

The twins had always had an uncanny way of knowing what the other was thinking, so their being on the same wavelength felt comforting and familiar. However, Michelle didn't know which was more surprising—that her children knew one end of a pot or pan from the other or that they wanted to invite Dave for dinner. She settled on the first one.

"You cook?" she asked.

"Of course, we cook." Ashley scoffed. "You don't think we've lived on takeout and fast food the past four years, do you?"

"Or that slop they served in the cafeterias on campus." Ashley turned up her nose. "Our first year at the university, we taught ourselves a few basic dishes."

"We had to if we were going to survive."

"We've gotten quite good at it," Ashley finished.

A heady mix of curiosity and temptation pulled at Michelle. As much as she wanted to see what her children could do in the kitchen, though, she knew better. Nina wouldn't appreciate it if the twins descended on her domain without warning. The chef might not say anything—she might just stew in silence—but it'd be better to give her friend a day's notice. Two would be even better.

"It's sweet of you to offer, but..." Michelle searched for an alternative. "What if we all go to Maggie's Diner for supper tonight and save your dinner for another time? We'll need to go to the big grocery store in Destin for supplies anyway." Her chicken parm called for a special cheese that Gus didn't stock at the Sugar Sand Grocery Store.

Aaron and Ashley's heads bobbed in unison.

"Sure. We can totally do that," Ashley agreed for both of them.

"I'll text Sara. See if she can join us." Aaron reached for his cell phone.

Michelle lifted an eyebrow. "You've stayed in touch with Sara?"

"Yeah. She's okay." Aaron's fingers flew over the keys.

While her son waited for a response, Michelle pinned her daughter with a quizzical expression.

Ashley shrugged. "She's nice. We like her."

"She'll be here." Aaron announced. His phone disappeared into a pocket.

Michelle jotted down a mental reminder to mention their children's friendship to Dave. Did he know? More to the point, did Aaron, Ashley and Sara discuss their parents like she and Dave discussed their children?

Not sure how she felt about that last thought, she surveyed the table. Gwen had removed their empty plates. The drinks she'd refreshed were nearly empty again. Michelle lay her hands flat on the wooden surface. "Why don't we get you settled in your rooms next. Erin and Reggie's parents arrived a couple of days ago. They're in the Manatee suite." Her daughter had stayed in those rooms on her previous visit. "If you don't mind, Ashley, I'll put you in the Dolphin this time. Aaron, you can have the Redfish again."

Ashley grabbed one of her hands. "Mummy, it doesn't matter where we stay. We'd sleep on the floor if we had to. We're just glad to be here and glad to see you doing so well."

Michelle reached for her children's hands. "You took the words right out of my mouth." There'd been a time when she'd feared Aaron and Ashley would never forgive her for the decisions she'd made following their father's death. But time had helped them move past their grief, and her friends had helped them overcome their anger. It had taken the better part of two years, but the twins were moving on with their lives and, finally, they recognized her need to move on with hers. All things considered, that was a very good thing.

Six

Reggie

*D*on't worry. Chris is double-checking the anchors on the swing set, and I'm going to take one last look around outside. Then we'll be right behind you."

"Aw-right. Parade starts at noon sharp. Don't be late." Jimbo gunned the engine of the now-empty van that had been filled to the rooftop with gifts when he pulled up in it this morning. The window on the driver's side glided shut.

Reggie pushed away from the vehicle she and Michelle, Erin and Nina had donated for Robert Phelps, Sugar Sand Beach's wounded warrior. She waved as the mechanic pulled out of the drive and joined the last of the volunteers. Jimbo, Reggie and Chris, along with a dozen other people, had spent the morning putting the finishing touches on the house the town had built for the veteran and his family. Most of the crew had spent hours arranging furniture, hanging curtains, and washing windows. As a result, everything inside the house was picture-perfect and ready for the arrival of the new owners.

She and Chris had been in charge of the exterior. Had they done their job as well as the other volunteers?

Reggie propped her hands on her hips and took a good, hard look around. An inviting yard filled with thick, healthy grass surrounded the sturdy concrete block and stucco house that sat well back from the street. A young bluejack oak stood proudly in the middle of the front lawn. In a few years, it would grow tall enough and wide enough to provide plenty of shade. Hardy plants and flowering bushes filled the well-mulched beds on either side of an extra wide sidewalk. An American flag hung from a pole over the front porch. The stars and stripes rippled in a light breeze.

Satisfied with the front, Reggie walked across the freshly mowed grass to the lawn mower. She pushed it into the fenced backyard, where a small shed held the basic gardening tools any homeowner would need. After wheeling the mower inside, she closed and latched the door.

She studied the backyard with a critical eye.

Here, as in the front, sloping sidewalks replaced stairs and made it easy for someone in a wheelchair to move in and out of the house without assistance. Three saplings had been planted in the backyard. In time, they'd create a shady bower for the children to play under. She crossed her fingers, hoping it would all meet the new residents' approval. Finally, her gaze landed on Chris, who stood beside one leg of the wooden swing set.

"You about done there?" she called.

Chris shoved his full weight against the set, which boasted two swings, a glider and a slide. It didn't budge. Moving to the attached playhouse, he tried and failed to knock it over. Stepping away, he rubbed his hands.

"You'd need an elephant to push this thing over," he declared. "A couple of little kids ought to be fine on it." Robert and his wife had two children—a seven-year-old boy and his four-year-old sister.

"I guess we're finished here, then. We probably ought to get moving. The parade starts in less than two hours." After working on the yard since shortly after sunrise, Reggie was looking forward to a nice, long shower. For that matter, Chris could use one, too, she thought, drinking in her fill of sweat-slicked skin and muscular arms. An image of them taking that shower together popped into her head, and she swallowed.

That so wasn't going to happen. At least not any time soon. Though she and Chris had both admitted their feelings for one another, they weren't in any rush. In fact, they hadn't actually gone out on a date yet. Oh, she'd had dinner at his house the other night while his mom played bingo at the Kiwanis Club with her friends. But by the time she and Chris got Hope fed and bathed and tucked into her crib with Binky, they'd had time for little more than a kiss or two before his mom's key rattled in the lock at the front door.

"You still want to watch the parade with me and Hope?" Chris asked as he strode toward her.

"I wouldn't miss it," she answered. A giddy thrill passed through her. Hope had babbled happily at the colorful lights and the shiny tinsel that hung throughout the inn. Reggie could hardly wait to see the toddler's expression when the little girl saw Santa on his sleigh.

As she and Chris headed through the gate and walked toward the street, he held her hand. She glanced at the tall man. "Are we still meeting in front of the community center at eleven thirty?"

"Sounds about right. Mom's taking Hope down early. She wants to make sure we have a good spot to watch the parade." His footsteps slowed. "Will that give you enough time?"

Reggie checked her watch. She'd have to hustle, but she'd make it.

Nearly two hours later, Reggie fretted that she might be late while her truck idled in a long line of cars waiting to make the final turn into Sugar Sand Beach. At last, she followed the directions of teenagers wearing bright orange jackets. They waved her toward a grassy field that already held a gazillion vehicles. Amazed at the number of people who'd come to see the parade, she joined the hurrying throngs of parents pushing strollers and holding the hands of excited youngsters on a rather long walk the rest of the way into town. As she neared the grocery store, she moved past sawhorses stretched across the road on both sides of the median. Wondering how she'd ever find Chris and Hope in the mob, she wove in and out of clots of people who jammed the sidewalks and spilled onto the street. More volunteers worked the edges of the crowd, urging everyone to stay behind chalk lines drawn on the blacktop.

Finally, she spotted Hope sitting on her daddy's shoulders up ahead and waved. Her heart melted a little when the child's face crinkled into a big, drooly smile as Reggie got closer.

"Hey, sweetheart," she called up to the baby.

"Tee. Tee," Hope cooed. Her eyes wide, she pointed as if she wanted to make sure Reggie saw the gaily decorated trees in the median.

"I do see them," Reggie said, matching the little girl's enthusiasm. "And in just a minute, we're going to see something else. A parade!"

The sound of drummers caught Hope's attention. Her head swung toward the staging area behind the hardware store at the opposite end of the street.

While the little girl was distracted, Reggie nudged Chris. "Hey," she said with a smile.

"Hey yourself," he answered. Without taking his hands off his daughter, he leaned far enough down to plant a kiss on Reggie's forehead.

Surprised by the gesture, she backed away a step.

Chris eyed her carefully. "Not the reaction I was hoping for," he murmured.

Reggie just stared at him. "People will talk,"

she whispered despite the spark of longing that warmed her middle. So far, they'd been careful to hide their deepening feelings from the town gossips, but a kiss in public—even a chaste one— announced to the world that they were a couple.

"Let 'em talk." Chris placed another kiss on the top of her head. "Mmmm. You smell good. Is that a new outfit?"

A heady swirl of emotions coursed through Reggie. Not quite ready to deal with them, she tugged on the hem of the bright red sweater she'd paired with black leggings and a long-sleeved shirt in a colorful Christmas print. "It's not too much, is it?" she asked.

"I like it," Chris said with a grin. "Besides, look around you. Everyone's got the Christmas spirit." Holding Hope in place with one large hand, he flicked the strand of blinking Christmas lights he wore around his neck. "I was beginning to think you weren't going to make it. What took you so long?"

"I had to park a half-mile from here." Reggie gestured toward the overflow parking area. "I had no idea the turnout would be this large."

"Word got around that our grand marshal is a wounded warrior. Several veterans' organizations showed up in support. Lots of servicemen and their families, too."

Now that Chris had mentioned it, there were far more clean-cut young men and women than normal standing about. And she'd never seen so many older men wearing black leather vests in town before. Looking closely, she saw that their jackets sported various military patches.

"Everybody loves a hero." Reggie placed a hand over her heart to acknowledge the huge debt she owed anyone who'd served their country. She was glad she'd been able to repay some small part of it by helping to donate the van to Sugar Sand Beach's own veteran.

Speaking of thanks, she also needed to thank the woman who'd arrived early enough to save them a coveted spot in front of the Community Center. "Where's your mom?" she asked.

"She's over there with Jack and Ruth and some of the others." Chris indicated the review stand at one end of the street. The lawn chairs clustered around it had been reserved for those who needed a little extra assistance. Reggie spotted Chris's mom sitting next to Ruth Bees and Jack Henson. The older gentleman wore a sweater that might have taken first place in an ugly Christmas sweater contest. She blew kisses at them and was tickled pink when Hope mimicked the motion.

At the stroke of twelve, a roar of motorcycle

engines rose above the sounds of people laughing and talking.

"Here we go," Chris said. A note of childlike excitement filled his voice. He swung Hope down off his shoulders and settled her at his hip.

He'd no more gotten his daughter situated than a dozen motorcycles emerged from behind the hardware store and pulled onto the main street. Two abreast, they slowly rolled down the road with their lights flashing. Metal gleamed and mirrors glinted as the members of the county's various law-enforcement units rode past.

One rider gunned his engine right in front of the spot where Reggie and Chris stood. The noise startled Hope, and the baby began to fuss. Reggie patted the child on the back. "It's okay." She leaned in close to whisper into Hope's ear. "They're gone."

"Guh?" Hope lifted her head.

Reggie's own head bobbed. "Gone," she repeated. She crossed her fingers and hoped that the little girl would be more impressed by the marching bands and the floats.

Finding out would have to wait until later though because, at that moment, a bright red convertible nosed around the corner of the hardware store. Posters on the car doors announced the arrival of the parade's grand marshals, and the crowd went wild. A cheer started at the far end of the street. Like a tidal wave, it pulsed from one end of town to the other. Throughout the gathering, men and women stood at attention. Those in uniform, and some who weren't, saluted.

Robert and Zoe Phelps sat holding hands atop the convertible's back seat. Dressed in matching jeans and white sweaters, the couple smiled and waved at the people gathered along the streets. Every so often, they'd point out friends or family members to one another or to their children, who stood in the floor well behind the front seats. The little girl waved and smiled just like her mother was doing, while the boy frowned as if he wasn't sure he liked being in the center of all the attention.

Thunderous applause continued to ripple through the crowd as the vehicle moved ever so slowly down the street. Seeing the young man who'd sacrificed so much for his country sent a jolt of patriotic pride through Reggie. She joined in giving Sugar Sand Beach's hometown hero a hearty round of applause. Beside her, Chris kept one arm firmly wrapped around his daughter while he, too, clapped and cheered. Meanwhile, Hope giggled and laughed and clapped her little hands together.

Recognition dawned on Robert's face when the car neared the Community Center. Aiming a finger at the man standing beside Reggie, the veteran lobbed an imaginary ball at Chris, who pretended to catch it in an imaginary mitt. The moment happened so quickly that Reggie barely absorbed the fact that the hand Robert aimed at Chris was a prosthetic before the vehicle had moved another twenty feet on down the road.

Reggie elbowed Chris lightly. "I didn't know you two knew each other."

"We don't really. I helped coach his Little League baseball team one season. That was"— Chris ran a hand through his hair—"hmm, twenty years ago?"

Warmth spread through Reggie's midsection at the thought that, one day, her memories of Sugar Sand Beach would stretch back for twenty years or more. Would Chris still play an important role in her life when that day came? She hoped so and gave his arm a squeeze.

The rest of the parade passed quickly. Hope didn't seem too interested in the high-stepping majorettes who led squads of baton-twirlers down the street. She did, however, like the bands. Her little mouth formed a round "O," and she bounced in Chris's arms as the local high school's brass and percussion unit played a lively rendition of "Frosty The Snowman." Reggie thought the baby might enjoy the briefcase drill team, too, but Hope ignored the antics of the men and women dressed in business suits and snuggled against her daddy's chest while colorful floats passed by unnoticed.

She didn't stir again until the strains of "Here Comes Santa Claus" filled the air. The sound floated out from speakers mounted in the bed of a dark green pickup truck that towed Santa's sleigh on a flatbed. According to Chris, the cheery red-and-gold contraption spent most of the year in Jack Henson's barn.

Hope leaned forward. "Saa—" She pointed at the man in the red suit.

Santa laughed and patted his belly while, much to the delight of the children in the crowd, Mrs. Claus tossed out handfuls of candy canes.

"Saa?" Hope asked as children scrambled for the treats. She looked expectantly at Reggie and then Chris. "Saa!" She pushed against Chris's chest and kicked her legs.

"I think she wants what they have," Reggie said, indicating the red-and-white striped candies.

"No sugar for you, sweet thing." Chris poked his daughter's little belly. "You're already sweet enough. How about a cracker instead?" He rooted around in the diaper bag on his shoulder until he came up with a plastic baggie filled with his daughter's favorite treats. Handing it to Reggie, he said, "Can you get a couple of those out for her? Then we'll mosey on over to the reviewing stand. I think there's gonna be some speeches and whatnot."

Of course there would. Events like today's didn't happen without someone saying a few words. Reggie would have known that even if she hadn't overheard Michelle practicing her own speech.

Though they hurried, by the time they joined the rest of the well-wishers a little farther down the street, Robert sat with military bearing in a wheelchair by the podium, his wife and children at his side. Applause that drowned out the speakers forced Mayor Maggie to keep things short and sweet as she presented the young veteran and his family with the proverbial keys to the city. The gesture was one Robert had in all likelihood expected, and he reacted with grace and dignity. He, likewise, kept his remarks short, but once he finished and grasped the hand rims of his wheelchair, Maggie stopped him. Grinning, the mayor scanned the crowd. She motioned for quiet, and this time, the throngs fell silent.

"There are just a couple more things, Robert," she said.

"Yeah, Robert. Just one," someone yelled.

"Or two," someone else added.

Laughter rippled through the crowd as confusion flickered across the young man's face. He motioned to his wife and children, who'd started walking toward the ramp. They quickly returned to his side. As they did, Robert and his wife exchanged questioning glances.

Watching them, Reggie smiled. She'd been certain that someone—Robert's mother or a close friend—would let at least one of their secrets slip. But unless Robert and Zoe possessed an acting talent no one knew about, they were still in the dark. Which made what was going to happen next all the more exciting. She peered over the shoulder of the person in front of her, eager to see what happened next.

At Maggie's gesture, Michelle joined her at the podium. While she added her own welcome to the mayor's, six or seven volunteers cleared a wide path in front of the stage. Driving the freshly washed and waxed van, Jimbo Dutton followed the men in the orange jackets. The mechanic braked to a stop just as Michelle got to the heart part of the speech Reggie had heard her practicing.

"And it just so happened that Nancy Simmons left this fully accessible van gathering dust in the garage of what is now the Sugar Sand Inn. We, and by we, I mean all of us—" Michelle waved a hand at the many well-wishers who crowded the street. "We'd all like you to have it." She stepped forward and pressed a set of keys into Robert's hand.

The young soldier sat in what Reggie could only call stunned silence for a long moment. Zoe's fingers tented over her mouth. Tears ran down her cheeks.

"I, uh, I don't know what to say," Robert said at last. "I never expected something like this." He clutched the keys to his chest. "Thank you." He turned to face the crowd. "Thank you all."

"Yes! Thank you," Zoe repeated. "Robert and I have been looking forward to coming home for so long. This incredible gesture only proves that moving back to Sugar Sand Beach was the right decision."

"Would you like to check out your new van?" Maggie asked. "Because, frankly, there's one more thing we have to show you. But to do that, we need you to take that vehicle for a little test drive."

Robert addressed the crowd. "You've all gone above and beyond already. This is enough. Seriously."

Someone in the crowd below shouted, "More,

more, more," and soon the chant reverberated up and down the street. Robert shrugged as if the matter had been taken out of his hands. With Zoe and his children only a few steps behind, he slowly rolled down the ramp and crossed to the van, where Jimbo waited. With a press of a button, the side door of the vehicle slid open and a ramp folded out. Robert hesitated long enough for his son to step forward and grasp the handles of the wheelchair. The boy said something that got lost in the noise of the crowd. Whatever it was, it did the trick, and with his son's "help," Robert rolled up the gentle slope and straight inside.

Once everyone was seated and belted into place, Jimbo climbed behind the wheel again for the short drive to Robert and Zoe's new home.

Maggie waited until the van had pulled away before she tapped the microphone. "You are all welcome to join us as we share our final surprise of the day with Robert and his family. However, we ask that no one approach the house and that everyone respect the Phelpses' privacy."

Reggie looked at Chris. "What do you want to do? Go or stay?"

Chris shifted Hope's little body. Once the excitement of the parade had passed, the baby had fallen asleep in his arms. He patted his daughter's tiny bottom. "Someone's had a big day already. Besides, Mom's driving to Jacksonville this evening. She wants to spend some time with her sister before Christmas. I need to see her off. How about you? Are you going?"

"Nah. I need to head back to the inn. We're supposed to go over the final plans for Erin's wedding tonight." Reggie eyed the crowd that surged toward the Phelpses' new home. "I'll give them a few days to get settled in. Maybe stop by one day next week to see if they want to know anything about taking care of the plants and the yard." This time of year, the lawn wouldn't need mowing again for a month or so.

"Well, in that case." Chris leaned down for a kiss.

Reggie met him halfway. When their lips met, his touch loosed a flock of butterflies in her midsection, which tempted her to change her plans. Resistance was difficult, but she forced her feet toward the distant parking lot while Chris headed in the opposite direction. She'd promised to meet with Michelle, Erin and Nina, and she'd keep her word, no matter how much she wanted to do something about her growing feelings for Chris.

Seven

Nina

Where's Erin?" Nina placed the charcuterie board onto the glass-topped table. In the center of the large wooden tray, spirals of sliced sausages wound around the cheeses she'd arranged in a sunburst pattern. Clusters of grapes, tiny cups of mixed nuts and heavenly-smelling dried fruits filled in the gaps. Sleeves of tasty crackers and a thinly sliced baguette stood on opposite sides. She wasn't at all surprised when Reggie started to help herself. She gently slapped the younger woman's hand. "Uh-uh," she warned. "Wait for everyone else."

"Sorry." Reggie gave a sigh worthy of a movie star, but she withdrew her fingers with a wry grin. "Erin and Ron were working on their vows in the apartment when I left. She'll be along in a minute."

"And Aaron and Ashley?" Nina glanced over at Michelle. She'd fixed enough goodies to feed a small army, plenty even if the twins put in an appearance.

"They met Dave's daughter in Destin for a night out on the town." Michelle sighed happily. "It's nice to see the three of them getting along so well." She turned to Reggie. "What about your folks?"

"After the parade, they followed the crowd to see the Phelpses' house. By the way, you looked great up there on the stage today." Reggie aimed the compliment at Michelle. "So poised and comfortable. Like you were used to speaking to thousands of people every day."

"You didn't see my hands shaking then?" Michelle's eyes went round. She shook her head, a move that sent the precisely cut ends of her hair swinging. "I'm so happy Robert and Zoe liked the van. Their reaction was touching, wasn't it?"

"Are you kidding? I was in tears." Reggie reached for the charcuterie board, seemed to think better of it and withdrew her hand. "Especially when their little boy helped wheel his dad into the van."

"I bet that went viral," Nina said.

Reggie laughed. "Look at you, talking like a teenager."

Nina rolled her eyes. "The benefits of hanging out with Megs and Lily." One of the benefits, anyway. She'd been surprised by how much she loved spending time with Zeke's daughters. They'd grown closer than she'd ever thought possible. Though she'd never take the place of their mother, she knew she wanted to be a part of their lives. To take them shopping for clothes, help them follow their dreams and maybe someday — many, many years from now — ooh and aah over the wedding dresses they chose.

Michelle tapped her fingers on her chair's armrest. "Sorry, but let's stay on track. Where are your folks now?" she asked Reggie.

"I think they were going to stop at Maggie's Diner for dinner." Her strawberry-blond curls falling softly about her shoulders, she checked her cell phone. "Oh, I have a text. They had to wait for a table, but they're eating now. They should be here in a half hour or so."

"Good," Michelle declared. She brushed her dark hair off her face and snuggled deeper into her jacket. "I have some stuff to go over with you before Erin or your parents show up."

Nina had intended to duck back inside to get

their drinks. Although she was eager to get the others' opinions on a new mulled wine recipe, she decided to wait until they heard what Michelle had to say. She curled up on the love seat beneath a tall propane heater that took the chill out of the wintry night's air. "Let's hear it," she said.

"First off, the turret is coming along beautifully. Zeke and his team just have a little bit more trim work to finish up on Monday. They're planning to paint Tuesday and Wednesday. The furniture will all be delivered on Thursday. That'll give me Thursday and Friday to hang curtains, make the bed and decorate."

"Don't forget," Nina cautioned. "We already have a lot planned for Friday. The rehearsal is at four, and the candlelight service starts at seven."

"I totally forgot about the rehearsal." Michelle's face fell. "That's going to be cutting it short."

"I'd offer to help, but I'll be in full-on wedding supper prep." Nina mentally scoured her busy cooking schedule for the week but couldn't free up any time to help with the decorating.

"Do you want an extra pair of hands?" Reggie asked. "Now that the weather's turned cooler, there's not much for me to do outside."

"Thanks." Relief softened Michelle's shoulders. "I could use your help hanging curtain rods and towel racks and such."

"Don't worry. We'll get it all done," Reggie said confidently. "I'd ask Chris to pitch in, but he's on baby duty all week. His mom went to Jacksonville for a few days."

"Speaking of Chris." Nina's big tabby paraded across the porch. Mr. Pibbs stopped at the foot of the love seat and mewed. Scooping him into her arms, she continued, "Did I see the two of you kissing at the Christmas parade?"

"Hey, you make it sound like we were sucking face like a pair of lovesick teenagers." Reggie's skin flushed to the roots of her hair. "It was just one little kiss. When we were leaving."

"Still." Nina finger-combed Mr. Pibbs's silky fur. "You know how gossip spreads around here. By now, word is all over town that you and Chris are seeing one another."

Reggie folded her arms and leaned back against the cushions of her chair. "I think that was the point."

"Oh?" Nina eyed her friend. Chris's wife had died mere hours after giving birth to Hope. As for Reggie, her ex had put her through an emotional wringer. "It's good to see that you're both ready to 'get back out there.'" She released her hold on Mr. Pibbs long enough to enclose that last bit in air quotes.

"We're still not ready to jump in with both feet, but I like Chris—a lot—and he apparently likes me enough to set tongues wagging all over Sugar Sand Beach." Reggie grinned.

Michelle leaned forward and embraced her younger friend. "As long as he makes you happy, I'm happy for you." She pulled back. "If that ever changes, you say the word, and we'll be all over him like…"

"Like cane syrup on Viola's biscuits," Nina finished. Her assistant cook had shown up with a bottle of the thick, dark syrup last week and treated them all to the Southern staple. Nina had promptly embraced it as her favorite new condiment.

"Ugh. Sticky," Reggie complained.

"Yep." Nina laughed. Although Erin and Michelle had sopped up every drop of the tasty liquid with their biscuits, Reggie hadn't been quite as fond of the syrup that was sweeter—and stickier—than molasses.

"Okay." Michelle checked her watch. "Back to the turret while we still have a few minutes." Erin still thought Zeke and his crew were transforming the space into a honeymoon suite, but she'd have to find out the truth sooner or later. Michelle cleared her throat. "When do we want to tell them about it? Before or after the wedding?"

"Oh, before, definitely," Nina blurted. When Michelle and Reggie immediately raised their eyebrows, she explained. "We don't want them to spend their honeymoon worrying about where they're going to live, do we? Don't we want to put their minds at ease about it so they can simply enjoy their time together?"

Reggie stretched. "That makes sense. I know Erin's been worried that they won't find a place to rent while they build their own house. If they ever find a piece of property they like enough to buy. They're having trouble with that, too."

"What if I wrap the key to the Oasis Suite like a Christmas present and put it under the tree for them, then?" Michelle suggested.

"I can make a little wooden fob to match the sign we'll hang on the door," Reggie offered.

"Christmas morning, then?" Nina asked. Once everyone was up and had had their coffee and something to tide them over, they'd exchange presents. After that, she'd turn the kitchen over to Viola and Ethan, who'd put the finishing touches on the wedding supper while the rest of the household shifted into wedding mode.

"Perfect." Michelle leaned forward, her hand raised to high-five Reggie and then Nina. When they'd finished, Michelle propped her elbows on her knees and cupped her chin in her hands. "Now that that's settled, I wanted to tell you about the items we found hidden in the turret."

"Oh, right! I've been wondering about it, but to be honest, I've been so busy in the kitchen these last few days, I really didn't have time to ask." She'd considered closing the cafe at the same time as the inn, but had decided to stay open until the week before the wedding. Which, as it turned out, had been a very smart business decision. The last couple of weeks, there'd been a steady line out the front door as practically everyone in town met at least one friend for a holiday lunch at the cafe. "So, what was all that stuff?"

"I found a note in the basket of the bicycle. Nancy wrote that the staircase had always been her favorite place in the house. As a child, she'd sit on the steps and read for hours. When she was in high school, she'd run up and down the staircase for exercise. After the accident, though, after she realized she'd never walk again, she said she couldn't bear to look at it. She had her staff pile all the things she couldn't use any more—her bike, plus a lot of mostly sports equipment—

around the steps. Then she hired a carpenter to wall it all off."

"How incredibly sad," Reggie mused.

"Or smart," Nina countered. When the others gave her sideways looks, she felt she needed to explain. "We all do it. If something or someone brings us down, we don't keep them around. We cut them out of our lives. Like I did with Toby. Or you did with that woman from your old neighborhood, Michelle. What was her name?" She looked expectantly at her friend.

"Frannie Dumont," she answered without the slightest hesitation.

Nina gestured with a thumb. "That's the one." Michelle had a reputation for long-suffering patience, but even her friendship with the divorcee had dried up under the woman's constant barrage of complaints and criticism.

"There's just one problem with that philosophy." Michelle pulled at her lower lip. "You can't get rid of all the Frannies. There's always a new one popping up. In Nancy's case, she could literally wall things off, but she couldn't get rid of all the bikes in town. Children still rode them to school. In her day, the newspaper carrier probably used one to deliver the morning paper. It'd be impossible to avoid them all."

Reggie shrugged. "Didn't Dave say she was a recluse? Maybe that's why. Maybe she closed herself off from the world so she wouldn't have to see other people doing things she couldn't do anymore."

"Now *that* would be a sad way to live." Michelle's eyes glistened.

Seeing her friend's tears, Nina reminded herself that they were speculating about Michelle's birth mother. It was time to move the conversation in a slightly different direction.

"We'll probably never know why Nancy retreated from the world like she did, but that didn't stop her from being a kind and generous person." Nina didn't have to look far for examples of the woman's generosity. "She donated money to the town, to the hospital in Destin." She pointed at Michelle. "She left this house to you. How many lives did she change because of all the things she did? The four of us certainly wouldn't be where we are right now if it hadn't been for Nancy Simmons."

That was especially true for her own life, Nina thought. When she'd lived in Virginia, she'd had to work from sunup to midnight just to keep a roof over her head. There'd been no time for relationships, no time to fall in love. If it weren't for Nancy Simmons's gift, she would never have had a chance to open a restaurant of her own. Much less met the man who filled her heart with joy.

Nina studied her friends and saw the same thoughts reflected on their faces.

"I'd raise a toast to Nancy, but I don't have a drink," Michelle said at last.

"You know what?" Nina asked, making a split-second decision. "I think we've waited long enough for Erin and her folks. Reggie, call your sister and tell her to get her tush out here. It's time to talk wedding."

"On it," Reggie said. She retrieved her phone from her back pocket.

"I'll get our drinks," Nina said. "Then we'll have that toast." She scooted Mr. Pibbs aside and sprang from her seat. As she did, a car turned in at the driveway. "Looks like Edwina and Frank are here," she noted.

As if Ron and Erin had timed their arrival, footsteps echoed from inside the house. Nina held the door for the couple before she headed down the hall. In the kitchen, the smell of spices, apple, wine and citrus mingled in a fragrant blend. She ladled the fruity mulled wine from the gallon pot she'd left barely simmering on a back burner of the big Aga range. Adding a spiral of orange peel to each mug, she placed

123

their drinks on a sturdy tray. By the time she made it back outside again, greetings had been exchanged and everyone had fanned out to the assorted couches and chairs. Noting that Mr. Pibbs had saved her place on the love seat, Nina passed the tray around before she took her own mug. Once she was settled with the big tabby on her lap again, she lifted her cup.

"Here's to Nancy Simmons," she said as they all raised their mugs.

"And to a wonderful wedding," Michelle added, wearing a happy smile.

An hour later, Nina surveyed what was left of the charcuterie board. Despite her fears that she'd fixed too much, the group had done some serious damage to it. Only a few scraps of cheese and two stray olives—one black and one green—remained. Seeing the latter, though, reminded her of the olive tapenade she wanted to serve, along with a number of other appetizers, at Erin's wedding supper. As all the best dishes did, the accompaniment began with roasted garlic, and she made a note to have Ethan make sure they had enough.

"Hey, Nina." Erin's fingers snapped.

Her head jerked. "What?"

"I asked if I'd overlooked anything. Or if there was something you wanted to add to the schedule."

Nina paired her best puppy-dog look with a sincere, "Sorry. My mind wandered." The glower she got in return made her question whether her usually calm and serene friend was turning into a bridezilla. She hurried to explain. "If it's any help, I was thinking about your wedding supper."

Erin's frown immediately dissolved. "No problem. Let me go over everything one more time." She ticked items off on her fingers. "Tomorrow, we have to be at the bridal shop in Destin for our final fittings at ten. Wednesday is the bachelorette party—unless you want to cancel it. You still haven't told us what we're going to be doing. Are you sure I'm not asking too much of you? We don't have to have it if you need extra time to prepare for Saturday."

"That's sweet but totally unnecessary," Nina replied. Erin had been dropping not-so-subtle hints about Wednesday's agenda for several weeks. "Everything's all set. The car service is sending someone to pick us up at nine. It's going to be a full day, so don't plan on being back here until after five."

"I can't convince you to tell us where we're going or what we're going to be doing?" Erin batted her eyelashes.

As if that would convince me to spill the beans. Nina laughed at the bride's attempts to dig for clues. She shook her head. "Not a chance. But I will tell you this—dress more like you're going to church than on a five-mile run."

"Good to know." Erin consulted a short list before she turned to Ron. "Do you know what you and the guys are doing for your bachelor party?"

Ron's nod was filled with confidence. "Deep-sea fishing." He pointed at Michelle. "Your friend Dave knew a guy who hooked us up." He grinned. "Pun intended."

"See?" Erin swung to Nina again. *"He* knows what *they're* doing."

"No comment." Nina zipped her fingers across her lips.

"Okay, be that way. But it's the last time I'll ask you to plan a bachelorette party for me." Donning her best imitation of a sulky child, Erin crossed her arms over her chest.

"I sincerely hope so," Nina shot back. She sweetened the barb with a smile. "And I mean that in the nicest way possible." Lifting her glass, she tipped it toward Erin and Ron. "To the happy-ever-after you both deserve."

"I'll drink to that." Leaning forward, Erin touched the rim of her mug to Nina's. "This is awfully good," she said after taking a long sip.

"Thanks. I've been working on this mulled wine recipe for a while. I think it might make a good winter replacement for Gulf Coast Sunset." Even sunny Florida had a few cold days, and the blend of hot wine and cider was perfect for nights like this one when there was a chill in the air.

As the conversation drifted from the wedding to the honeymoon and a scuba-diving trip to look for sunken treasure the couple planned to make, Nina smiled. Erin's playful prying aside, she'd say one thing for her friend—Erin was no bridezilla. The delivery van from Polly's Posies could bring poinsettias instead of white roses, and Erin would take the change in plans in stride.

Was that what it was like when you knew you were marrying the right person? Nina thought it might be. For a brief moment, she imagined what it'd be like if she ever decided to take the marital plunge. Would she be so in love that, like Erin and Ron, it wouldn't matter whether she walked down an aisle or a staircase? Would the size of the bridal party, the floral arrangements, the venue amount to more than a hill of beans? Or would she be content to celebrate the occasion with good friends, good food—a must because every wedding should be celebrated with a great meal—and the man she loved?

Yep, she told herself. That was all she wanted.

Now she just had to find the right man. She closed her eyes for a long moment. Zeke's strong hands and wide shoulders were all she could think about. He was one in a million, always encouraging, never demeaning. He showered both her and his daughters with kindness and tenderness. And the more time she spent with him, the more she wanted to spend a lifetime in his arms.

The flash of headlights pulled her out of a very pleasant dream of a day in the not so distant future. Her eyes flew open. She blinked, trying to wrap her head around the fact that Chris had stepped out of his pickup truck and was unbuckling his daughter from her car seat.

She aimed her chin at Reggie, who hadn't seen the vehicle. "What's Chris doing here this late?"

The younger woman was on her feet in an instant, a concerned expression shaping her finely chiseled features. She spun toward the front of the house. "Chris?" she called. "Is everything all right?"

"Hey." The man exhaled a long breath. "Everything's fine. Well, we're fine," he corrected. "We just, uh… We need a place to stay." With a wailing baby propped against his chest, he approached the steps. His voice rose above Hope's plaintive cries. "I know it's the Christmas season and you're closed, but I'm hoping there's room at the inn?" His inquiring glance landed on Michelle.

Cushions rustled and chairs complained as the focus of everyone on the porch shifted to the new arrivals. Reggie hurried to Chris's side and took the fussy baby. "There, there." She patted the little girl's back, and Hope immediately quieted. Reggie continued to murmur soothing sounds to the child.

Nina nodded when Michelle looked to her for an answer. Erin did, too, and their official hostess cleared her throat.

"Of course, you're welcome here, Chris," she said. "But what's going on?"

"A water pipe broke under the kitchen sink," he said heavily.

Both Ron and Frank loosed sympathetic groans. The older gentleman turned to his wife. "Remember when that happened at our house?"

"What a mess," Edwina said sympathetically. "It took weeks to repair the damage. And we lost that Oriental rug Erin sent us from Thailand. I always liked that rug."

"Yeah, that's about right." Chris kicked a loose piece of gravel. "I came home from the parade to find an inch of water standing in my kitchen and living room. I've been sweeping water out the back door ever since while I tried to salvage as much as I could. The hardwood floors are a total loss. The bedrooms weren't touched, thank goodness, but there's no power until I can get an electrician to make sure nothing shorted out. I'd rough it if it was just me, but Hope can't stay there."

"Of course not." Michelle tsked as if the idea was out of the question. "What about your mom? Where is she?"

"She's in Jacksonville," Reggie reminded them in a soft whisper.

"She left to visit her sister this afternoon. I spoke to her. She's gonna stay there till the house is livable again."

"Well, let's see," Michelle said, apparently thinking aloud. "Where should we put you? Will

Trout be all right? Zeke and his crew still have a couple of days' work to do on the turret. But I hate to put you upstairs now that Hope is walking. Trout is on the first floor, and we have a portable crib she can use."

Nina winced. She'd never had kids, but the idea of turning an active toddler loose in a house full of breakables had to be a disaster in the making. They'd have to watch the little girl like a kettle of hawks to make sure she didn't get hurt.

"What if we moved them into the apartment instead?" Reggie suggested.

"What?" Nina felt her eyes widen. She understood that Chris and Reggie had grown close, but were they already thinking of moving in together?

"Now, now. Here me out," Reggie said. "I'm not suggesting that they stay *with* me. It's just that I've been babysitting Hope a little bit, so I've moved all the breakables and poisons out of reach of little hands." She shot a questioning look at her sister. "Would that be okay with you, Erin? You and I could move upstairs for now, couldn't we?"

Erin shrugged. "Fine with me." She rose. "Let me get some of my things."

"I'll go with you." Reggie turned to Chris. "It won't take us long to pack. As soon as we finish, you can move on in and stay as long as you need to."

"I hate to put y'all out. Especially with the wedding right around the corner." Chris looked at the bride-to-be.

"Don't worry about it." Erin rushed to reassure the man who was temporarily homeless. "I was planning to move in another week, and I've got most of my stuff all packed and ready to go anyway."

"Then it's settled." Reggie kissed the top of the baby's head.

"Well, there is one more thing. I hate to ask, but can you watch Hope tomorrow so I can meet with the electrician and call the insurance company?"

When Reggie hesitated, Nina felt the need to put her foot down. "You can't. We're going to the bridal salon with Erin. She has her final fitting, and we're supposed to try on our dresses."

"Uh." Reggie's weight shifted.

"Don't even think about canceling." Edwina spoke up from where she and her husband sat. "Frank and I can watch Hope tomorrow. That way you girls can go on to the fitting, and Chris can get things settled in the apartment and do whatever he needs to do at his house."

"That's very kind of you, ma'am, but..." Chris's voice trailed off.

His reluctance to leave his child with near strangers—even if they were Reggie and Erin's parents—was so apparent that it stirred months-old memories of when they'd first met and how careful Chris had been to always keep his daughter in his sight. "Viola will be here," Nina offered. She knew Chris trusted the assistant cook.

"Aaron and Ashley will be here to help out, too," Michelle added. "You'll be leaving your little girl in good hands, Chris."

"Yes, ma'am. Thank you." He nodded to Edwina. "And now, if you don't mind, I'd like to get this little one settled in for the night." He held out his hands to Hope, who reached for him. "She's had a long day."

"You have any bags in the truck?" Ron asked. When Chris admitted that he did, Erin's fiancé said, "I'll bring them in. Then I need to take off. I have a few things I need to take care of in the morning."

The offer signaled an end to the evening, and in minutes, the porch had cleared, people going off in different directions. Nina hefted the large, wooden serving platter and headed for the kitchen, where Michelle was loading mugs into the dishwasher.

"So much for closing the inn over the holidays," Nina murmured as she scraped the remains of the snack into the trash.

"You can say that again." Chuckling, Michelle shook her head. "What with the Bradshaws and the twins, and now Chris and Hope, and Erin and Reggie moving into the suites upstairs, nearly every room is taken.

"I'll be busier than ever, trying to keep everyone fed." Nina's mouth twitched. "And isn't that just what we wanted?"

"I've always loved having a houseful at the holidays," her friend said with a wistful smile. "You know, last year, I couldn't have imagined any of this." She moved her arm in a sweeping gesture. "But you and Erin and Reggie lifted me out of a dark place, and coming here has given me hope for a brighter future than I ever thought possible."

"I couldn't have said it any better," Nina agreed. Thanks to the best friends a girl could ever want, she'd been given a second chance to do what she loved doing with people she cared about and a man who meant more to her every day. Who could ask for more?

Eight

Erin

The sun still hid below the horizon when Erin padded, barefoot, into the kitchen to get a drink of water before her morning run. With the cafe closed until after the first of the year, she didn't expect to see anyone else this early. Movement in the shadowy depths of the breakfast nook made her jump. She peered closely.

"Mom?" Edwina Henson was not known as an early riser. "What are you doing up already?"

"I couldn't sleep, honey." Edwina lifted a steaming mug to her lips and sipped.

Erin stiffened. Tea was her mom's comfort beverage, something she only drank when she was deeply troubled. And then, only with plenty of milk and sugar. Judging from the number of empty white packets and used tea bags sitting on the saucer on the table, her mom hadn't slept a wink all night.

Instantly hitting the "pause" button on her plans for an early run, Erin slid onto the bench seat. "What's bothering you? Is something wrong with Dad? Are you ill?" She suppressed a shiver. She'd reached the age where having both her parents in her life was no longer guaranteed. Not that it had ever been.

"No, we're fine." Edwina patted her hand. "Your dad passed his physical with flying colors last month. My doctor says I'll probably live to be a hundred."

Well, that was one less thing to worry about. Erin let her pent-up worries escape in a long breath.

"What about money? Are you having problems?" Her father had all kinds of stock options and a healthy 401K when he retired, but in this day and age, scammers could empty someone's accounts before they even knew about it.

A few strands of fine, gray hair had worked loose from Edwina's usual up-do. Her movements self-conscious, she attempted to tuck them back in place as she said, "It's not your father and me I'm worried about. It's you."

"Me?" Erin rocked back. She'd probably given her parents more than enough sleepless nights over the last forty-five years. But now, when she'd finally settled down, when she was doing what she loved to do with people she enjoyed being around, when she was marrying the one man she'd always loved, why would her mom be worried about her now?

Her elbows on the table, Edwina folded and re-folded her hands several times. At last, in a thin voice, she asked, "Are you sure this is what you want, Erin?"

"To marry Ron? To live in Florida? To help run the inn?"

Her mom's lips pressed together in a firm line.

"I'm not trying to be difficult, but I'm not sure what you're asking. Can you give me a hint?" Erin studied her mother's face.

"It's this wedding. Are you sure you want such a..." Edwina paused, clearly groping for the right word. "Such a small wedding?" she finished.

Erin expelled a thready breath. *The wedding.* Of all the troublesome things in the world, her mom should not spend a minute, much less a sleepless night, fretting about her wedding. "Uhhh. Yeah. It's what we planned, Ron and me. Something small and simple, but, you know, elegant."

"I'm just not sure it's the right thing." Edwina shook her head. "You and Ron practically eloped last time. Your father and I were hoping you'd let us pull out all the stops for you this time. You know—white doves and flower girls. A reception at the Elks Club with all our friends and family there."

"Are you saying that's what you want? A big whoop-de-do? 'Cause it's a little late to plan a big wedding, isn't it? I mean, I'm getting married in six days." She wanted to tread lightly here. She might have reached her mid-forties, but that didn't mean she had outgrown her need for her parents' approval. Before she said "I do," she wanted, needed their blessing.

"What's the rush? If you waited until spring or next summer, we could plan a proper wedding. Your dad and I would pay for everything…" Edwina's hands twisted again. Her tone took on a quality Erin had never heard her mother use before. "Don't you and Ron want a big celebration? Like we gave Reggie and Sam? I've always felt bad that we didn't do the same for you. Like we let you down."

The pleading look in her mother's big blue eyes fairly gutted her, but she had to make her mom understand. "It's not the size of the guest list that we care about. It's what's in our hearts. I love Ron, and he loves me. We've already spent too many years apart. We don't want to waste another day. Certainly not another six months." Erin waited a beat. So far, they'd been talking about the size of the wedding. But was that all that was bothering her mother? Was she questioning Erin's decision to get married at all? Or was it the fact that she was marrying Ron? Whatever the cause, Erin couldn't allow those doubts to fester.

"Um, look, Mom. I hate to ask, but you're happy about me and Ron getting back together again, aren't you?" She didn't wait for an answer but rushed on. "'Cause I don't have any doubts. As soon as we reconnected, I felt whole for the first time since our divorce. He completes me. I do the same for him. I love him so much that I almost walked away from all of this." She rapped lightly on the tabletop. "But he loves me too much to let me do that. Instead, he sold his house and his business in Houston, packed up all his belongings and moved here. To be with me. If that's not true love, I don't know what is."

"Oh, Erin." Edwina sniffed.

Erin stared at her mom. Were those tears? Her mother didn't cry. Not ever. But that was definitely a fat tear trickling down her mother's cheek. That settled it. She captured her mom's wandering hands. "Who are you, and what have you done with my mother?" she asked.

Edwina laughed through her tears. "Oh, honey. Your dad and I have been so worried. When you first told us you and Ron were getting back together, we were so happy for you. But then, when we got here, you two were acting more like good friends than lovers. This—what you just said—it makes all the difference. I can rest easy now that I know in my heart that you and Ron are marrying for the right reason. For love."

Erin pulled her mom into a fierce hug. When they pulled back, she said, "Well, if you're going to rest, you'd better do it now. It's almost five. In less than four hours, Michelle, Nina, Reggie and I have to leave for our dress fittings. You're going to have to be on your toes if you're going to watch Hope."

"Not to worry." Edwina brushed Erin's concerns aside. "Your dad and I are old hands at taking care of babies and such. You know we run the nursery at church back home. Some Sundays, we have more than ten toddlers in our class. We'll take great care of that little girl." She paused.

Erin could practically see the wheels turning in her mother's head.

"But speaking of Hope," Edwina continued, "what's going on with Reggie and her father?"

Erin smiled. "That's something you'll need to ask my sister, but I'll tell you this much... Ron and I have a little wager going on which of them will walk down the aisle next—Michelle and Dave, Nina and Zeke, or Reggie and Chris. Want to know who my money's on?"

"Nope." A broad smile on her face, Edwina stood. "Don't tell me. Let me watch them this week, and then I'll make my own predictions. For now, though, I think I'll take your advice and toddle off to bed for a couple of hours."

She started to gather up her tea things, but Erin stopped her. "I'll get those, Mom. But Mom..."

"Yes, honey?"

"Are you sure you don't want to come with us to the bridal salon?" She'd asked her when her mom and dad first arrived, but Edwina had turned down the offer.

Edwina's soft hands cupped Erin's shoulder. "Thanks, but I'll wait to see you in your gown on your wedding day. For now, I'm off to beddy-bye. I'll rest easy knowing you and Ron belong together."

Her movements as graceful as they'd ever been, Edwina headed down the hall. A few minutes later, Erin heard her mother's footsteps on the stairs. She tightened her ponytail. Sometime today, she'd have to warn her sister that, wherever she went, whatever she did, their mother was watching.

Nina barely glanced at the interior of the car as she slid onto the plush leather seat. "Whose idea was it to put off our final fittings until the week before the wedding?" she complained. "I really can't afford to take the time off for this."

"Tell me about it," Michelle said. She took her place beside Nina. "I certainly hadn't planned on having a full house this week. It's really thrown my schedule off kilter."

"I feel like I'm constantly putting out fires," Reggie added. She scooted past the small table in the center of the limo and sat facing Nina. "I should stay home today and look after Hope." She cast a longing glance out the window.

"Don't even think about getting out of this car," Erin ordered. "Mom and Dad are perfectly capable of watching after one baby." She pinned her sister with a look that was all business.

Next, she turned to Nina. "I wouldn't bat an

eyelash if you served hot dogs and hamburgers on Saturday. I appreciate that you want to make our wedding supper something special, but there's no need to stress about it."

Finally, she addressed Michelle. "Yes, we have a houseful. And no, we didn't plan it that way, but they're all family. Think of it as a reunion. No one expects to be waited on hand and foot, like some of our paying guests do."

Good grief. She was the bride. She was supposed to be tense. But everyone around her was more on edge over the wedding than she was.

Behind her, the limo driver closed the door. Knowing there was no escape for her friends or her sister, Erin relaxed. She reached for the bottle of champagne chilling in the ice bucket and poured a generous serving into each of the four flutes the driver had provided. After topping off the glasses with freshly squeezed orange juice, she lifted one.

"Cheers," she said, firmly reminding her bridesmaids that this was supposed to be a happy occasion.

Although Nina, Michelle and Reggie grumbled a bit more, they raised their glasses before each retreated to their own thoughts. Erin sighed. Sinking into the soft leather seat, she sipped her mimosa. The silence that filled the car was better than listening to her friends' complaints, she supposed. However, the day wasn't exactly turning out the way she'd thought it would. She tucked one hand out of sight, her fingers crossed. Hopefully, the surprise she'd planned at the bridal salon would lift everyone's spirits.

"Erin?" Confusion laced the voice coming from one of the dressing rooms in It's All About The Dress.

Erin crossed her legs and let her shoe dangle from the tips of her toes. As she'd requested, the ever-helpful Gretta had hung Michelle, Reggie and Nina's bridesmaids' gowns in three separate dressing rooms before their limo arrived at the doorstep of the house that had been converted into the best bridal salon in the area. Claiming she wanted to get the full effect of seeing them in their gowns all at once, Erin had asked her friends to try on their dresses at the same time.

"Yeah?" She clamped one hand over her mouth. The urge to giggle nearly overwhelmed her, but determined to continue the ruse for as long as possible, she swallowed her laughter. "Is there a problem?" she asked, trying her best to sound innocent.

"I, uh... I'm not sure this is the gown I ordered. The color's wrong, and the dress..." Nina's voice faded into what Erin could only assume was shocked silence.

Reggie's surprised gasp rose from another dressing area. Her hair a mass of curls tumbling around her shoulders, she opened the door just wide enough to peek her head out. "I don't think this is right. Gretta, could you check the tag on mine?"

"I personally double- and triple-checked the order forms and the dresses when they arrived." Wearing a simple black pantsuit that stood out in the sea of white gowns that filled the salon, the sales clerk maintained her usual calm demeanor despite the humor that glinted in her eyes.

"There are a lot more layers than I remember." A rustle of fabric muffled Nina's complaint.

"I'm sure, whatever the problem is, our seamstress can handle it in alterations," Gretta soothed while Erin fended off another round of giggles.

"I beg to differ." Michelle's uncharacteristically firm tone came from yet another dressing room. She stepped out onto the carpeted runner that led to a raised dais and a three-way mirror.

Erin fumbled for her phone, anxious to record the image of her friend wearing poufy sleeves and a dangerously low décolleté that arrowed into a waspish waist above a skirt that consisted of acres of shiny pink satin.

Nina emerged from her room wearing a similar confection in pale lavender. "I thought we all decided on sage green," she said. Her voluminous skirt swished.

"Really, Nina? That's what you're concerned about? The color? Not this?" Michelle pointed to the ribbons and bows that adorned practically every inch of her dress.

"I know the one I picked out didn't have these sleeves." Plucking at pale yellow fabric that ballooned at each of her shoulders, Reggie joined Michelle and Nina. "And with this hair, I'd never have chosen yellow."

"Oh. My. Word." Unable to locate her hips under the masses of fabric, Nina settled for placing her fists in the general vicinity. She swung on Erin. "What have you done?" she demanded.

Her body trembled as laughter boiled up within her. "You should see your faces. Priceless," Erin declared. Her friends' reaction was everything she'd hoped for. Snapping pictures as fast as she could, she didn't bother to hold back her laughter anymore. The sight of her three besties dressed like Southern belles on their way to a ball was hilarious. Her laughter was contagious, and soon, everyone had a bad case of the giggles. Even the normally serene Gretta chortled.

"So these aren't the dresses we're wearing for the wedding," Michelle clarified when she could catch her breath.

"Goodness no, dear," Gretta explained. "These lovely gowns are for the Camellia Festival at the Wesley House." Built in the 1890s, the antebellum-style mansion housed one of the largest collections of Louis XVI furniture in the US. This year's festival coincided with a milestone anniversary, and docents in period attire would give tours of the extensive flower gardens that peppered the grounds.

Reggie spun in a circle. The hem of her gown flared out. "I don't know. I think we should keep them. I can see you greeting guests at the inn in that dress, Michelle."

"They are very well made," Michelle allowed. "The trim is exquisite. But I can't quite see Nina wearing satin when she's working in the kitchen. Those skirts alone would be a fire hazard."

The comment loosed another round of schoolgirl-like giggles. Only Gretta remained sober. The sales clerk coughed into one hand. "I'm afraid these particular gowns aren't for sale," she said carefully.

"Relax. They're not serious," Erin assured her.

"When have we ever been serious?" Nina asked as she tugged the ponytail holder from her hair and let the long, dark strands fan out over her shoulders.

"Eh, once in a while we get too serious," Michelle answered. She turned to the bride-to-be. "This was a good one, Erin. You had me going there for a minute."

Erin adjusted the diamond ring on her finger. A rare vibe had filled the inn lately. Michelle fretted about the unanticipated company they were hosting over the holidays. Nina was so concerned about the wedding supper, she could hardly think of anything else. Reggie scurried from project to project. She'd hoped the practical joke would unknot the tension that surrounded even her simple wedding.

"I just want us to have fun on Saturday. I know we've all been working hard to make things perfect, but really, love and laughter are all that matters." Suddenly teary-eyed, Erin took a breath. "Now let's get a few more pictures, and then we'll settle down to business. We actually do have a fitting today."

Reggie hopped up on the dais, where she fanned herself with one hand. "Why, I de-clare," she said, stretching out each syllable. "That Ron fella is so fine, I could just swoon."

Nina stepped up beside Reggie. She pressed the back of one hand to her forehead. "Is it hot in he-ah, or is it just me?" she asked, following Reggie's example.

"Now, Miss Erin." Michelle took up the cause. "Y'all be careful now or you gonna end up getting' yourself some gooood lovin'." When she pursed her lips over her open palm and blew kisses, Nina and Reggie did the same.

Erin captured the image of the three of them in mid-kiss and knew instantly the picture was a keeper, one she'd always treasure. Handing her phone to Gretta, she joined her friends on the dais, where they mugged for the camera while the clerk took a few more pictures.

"I guess we'd better get serious now," she said at the first sign that the joke had run its course.

By the time Nina, Reggie and Michelle returned to their dressing areas and shimmied out of the oversize frocks, Gretta had emerged from the back room of the salon with a rolling clothes rack. She swapped the poufy confections for sage green gowns with slim-fitting skirts. Not wanting to be too matchy-matchy—a fashion faux pas of the highest order, according to Michelle—they'd chosen a basic style that came with a variety of options. Nina's featured a sleeveless bodice that hugged her ample curves, while Michelle had gone with slightly more conservative cap sleeves that looked adorable on her. Reggie landed somewhere in the middle with a sweetheart V-neck and thin shoulder straps.

Once everyone had given their gowns a hearty stamp of approval, it was time for the moment of truth. Erin slipped into her own dressing room to try on the wedding dress she'd selected. When she and Ron had exchanged vows at the courthouse all those years ago, she'd worn a sundress of white eyelet that she'd bought off the rack at her local department store. This time, knowing her marriage would last forever, she'd splurged on the dress of her dreams.

If she had any doubts about her wedding gown, the oohs and aahs of her friends as she stepped out of the dressing room put those fears to rest. She'd been going for a simple yet elegant look in keeping with the rest of the wedding. The classic lines of the off-white dress delivered it in spades. The V-neck showed just the right amount of cleavage. The bodice hugged her close before flaring out into a full skirt. With heels, the hem barely brushed the tips of her toes.

"I absolutely adore it," Reggie gushed. "That fabric—what is it? It's gorgeous."

"Mikado silk," Erin answered. She skimmed her fingers lightly over the fabric, which had been imported from Italy. Despite its heavy weight, it felt satiny cool to the touch.

"Ron is going to lose his mind when he sees you in that dress," Michelle said with solemn assurance.

Nina crossed both of her hands over her heart. "It's perfect," she declared.

It was, and Erin wished she never had to take it off. At last, though, she reluctantly exchanged the gown for her street clothes. After receiving repeated assurances from Gretta that their dresses would be delivered to the inn the following day, she and her friends piled back into the limo for a far more enjoyable ride home.

Nine

Nina

On Wednesday, the party bus braked to a smooth stop in front of The Gulfside Spa. The instant the driver opened the doors, Nina scrambled from her spot in the first row. Turning to the sea of faces that bobbed in the leather seats, she homed in on the blonde wearing a bedazzled white baseball cap.

"Our first stop," Nina said. Taking a breath to quell a sudden rush of nervous energy, she pointed to a chalkboard on the sidewalk. The sign had been decorated with hearts and wedding rings. In swirly letters, it welcomed Erin and her party to the spa. A moment later, a woman dressed in soothing green tones stepped onto the sidewalk and beckoned the guests.

Beneath the cap that identified her as the

bride, Erin clutched her fisted hands to her mouth and squealed. "I was sooo hoping for a spa day!" Excited chatter spread from seat to seat, echoing the sentiment.

Relieved that her choice for the outing had met with such enthusiastic approval, Nina grabbed an oversize tote bag filled with snacks and bottled water from an empty seat and dashed down the stairs.

Megan and Dimella were the first off the bus. Nina handed the girls a sheet of pink card stock that listed the age-appropriate spa services they could enjoy. The adults would receive cream-colored cards with a more extensive offering, one that included six different massages and several waxing options.

"But I'm nearly grown," Megs protested as she scanned a menu that included mani-pedis, leg and arm massages, and cucumber facials. "I want a real massage." She aimed a hopeful glance at Nina. "And a wax."

As hard as it was to deny the girl anything, Nina forced herself to stay strong. "In a few years, with your mom and dad's approval, you and I can schedule a full spa day, just the two of us. But for now, we'll stick with this list." She had no intention of letting anyone give Megs a rubdown any more than she'd dream of taking a waxed twelve-year-old home to her father. She kissed the girl on the top of her head and drank in the fragrance of frangipani and jasmine that rose from the leis she'd handed to everyone as they boarded the bus earlier.

Megs heaved a sigh and rolled her eyes at Dimella, who waited for her on the sidewalk. "I had to try."

"Told ya she wouldn't go for it," said Charlie and Viola's slightly older, slightly wiser daughter. The two girls linked arms. Just before they disappeared inside the spa, Dimella said, "We'll still have fun. Come on. We'll pick out really cool colors for our nails."

"Girls. Always pushing to be grownups. If they only knew how much easier they have it now, they wouldn't be in such a hurry," Viola said as she stepped off the bus.

"Ain't that the truth," Nina agreed. "I wish we could get it through their thick skulls to slow down and enjoy life. Figure out who they are and what they want before they rush headlong into adulthood."

Viola took the card Nina handed her. "There's no prices on this list," she pointed out. A rare frown crossed her lips.

Nina leaned in close enough to whisper, "We have an in with the owner—Miss Polly's son,

Walt." The man was a millionaire several times over, thanks to an app he'd sold to a major corporation. He'd invested part of his money in businesses throughout Panama City. "Not only did he make me a deal I couldn't refuse, he arranged for us to have the spa all to ourselves this morning." Which was pretty decent of him considering he'd been sweet on Erin ever since they met at the Fourth of July craft fair.

"You're sure?" Viola's frown deepened.

"Absolutely," Nina assured the woman, who was both a friend and an employee.

"Okay, then. You don't have to tell me twice." Her hips swaying, Viola followed her daughter and Megs into the salon.

Looking like a startled fawn, Lily had frozen halfway down the steps of the bus. Behind her, Ashley waited patiently.

"C'mon, sweetie," Nina coaxed.

Lily hesitated a moment longer before, taking one tentative step at a time, she joined Nina on the sidewalk.

"You okay?" Nina asked. Lily was practically fearless in the kitchen. It wasn't like her to be reluctant to try something new.

"I heard Megs and Dimella talking about getting their eyebrows plucked. With tweezers." Lily's eyes grew damp. "Daddy uses tweezers when he pulls splinters out of my fingers. I don't like it. Is this gonna hurt?"

"Oh, gosh, no." A fierce protectiveness washed through Nina. She pulled the little girl into a reassuring hug. Lily was such a remarkable cook, sometimes she forgot the child was only eleven. "Today is all about making us feel special, pampered. No one is going to hurt you."

Ashley joined them. "Hey, kiddo," she said, leaning down to Lily. "I could use a spa partner. Will you be mine? We'll get our nails done. I'm not sure about my feet, though." She wiggled her toes in her sandals. "I'm ticklish. How about you? Do you want to get your toes painted?"

"I like it when Megs or Mommy paints my nails," Lily allowed. She held out one hand. Four of the five fingers bore the chipped remains of sparkly pink polish.

"Well, that settles it." Ashley tucked the little girl's hand in the crook of her arm. "The manicure station will be our first stop." Her voice dropping as if she was sharing a secret, she said, "Now, when we go inside, the first thing the lady will say is, 'Pick your color…'"

Lily threw a smile over one shoulder at Nina as she skipped off with her new "partner."

"That was sweet," Michelle said, watching

them go. "I have to admit it, that daughter of mine has given me a few gray hairs. It's nice to see how well she's turning out."

Nina nodded. She and Erin and Reggie had worried right along with their friend. "I like that she took Lily under her wing without even being asked. She's got a good head on her shoulders, that one. Like her mama." Smiling, she handed Michelle the list of spa services. "What are you going to do first?"

"I'd love to get a massage, if there's time." Michelle bit her bottom lip the way she often did when uncertainty plagued her. "But with so many of us…"

"No problem. We'll be here for three hours, and the manager assured me that they'll have a full staff on hand to take care of all our needs."

"That's good. Thanks so much for setting all of this up, Nina."

"Yeah, thanks," Reggie added. She bounced Hope on one hip as Erin and their mom joined them. "This is much better than anything I would have come up with."

"What's that?" Erin wanted to know.

"Oh, I don't know. Water skiing? Parasailing? Skydiving?"

"Three days before my wedding?" Erin managed to looked shocked. "That's all I'd need—

I'd break my leg and be in a cast the entire honeymoon."

"Which is exactly why we put Nina in charge of today's activities," Reggie pointed out.

"You don't mind that we included the girls on your special day, do you?" Nina's gaze took in the drooly baby Reggie held. She'd fretted over the decision to bring the children along.

Erin adjusted her ball cap. "I would have suggested it, but I wasn't sure what you'd planned for us."

Oh, so the bride was still miffed about not knowing the plans ahead of time, was she? Wait till she saw what came next.

Pretending to overlook the dig, Nina explained her reasoning. "The way kids are glued to social media these days, I'm pretty sure Dimella and Megan, at least, think a bachelorette party has to be one of those wild nights in Vegas or Atlantic City. I wanted them to see what real women do. We don't need strippers or tequila shots to have a good time." Besides, what choice did she have? She couldn't very well ask Edwina and Viola to babysit; Erin's bachelorette party wouldn't be complete without them. Chris and Zeke couldn't watch the children; they and the rest of the guys had gone deep-sea fishing. A boat in the middle of the Gulf was no place for an active toddler.

"Wait. What? No shots? No strippers?" Erin feigned a horrified expression that quickly melted into laughter. Nina joined in along with Reggie, Michelle and Edwina.

The oldest of the group sobered first. "A little pampering goes a long way," she said. "Speaking of which, I'm going to see if anyone can give me a pedicure. It's been so long since I've had one that my calluses have calluses."

"And I want to see a girl about some wax." Erin casually swept her hand below her waist.

The motion loosed another round of laughter as they moved inside. For the next three hours, they let themselves be pummeled and plucked and, as if that wasn't enough, had hot wax ripped from their bodies...all in the name of beauty. And they enjoyed every minute of it.

At their next stop, Chef Charlie had reserved one of the Happy Dolphin's private rooms for their lunch. White twinkle lights hung from the ceiling in graceful loops. The lights turned the room into a winter wonderland. To further the image, Nina had dressed the tables in white linens. At Viola's urging, Dimella owned up to tucking miniature Christmas trees into the elegantly folded napkins on each plate. The young girl glowed when the rest of the party praised her contribution. On a side table, dark green fondant covered the cake Viola had baked for the occasion. She'd adorned it with a bridal gown of creamy white fondant that looked so real, Nina was tempted to run her fingers over the skirt.

Once they were seated, a pair of waiters circulated about the room, filling glasses with wine for the adults and cider for the children who'd clustered together at one end. Sitting beside Erin at the head of the long table, Nina raised a glass in a toast to the bride. Edwina and Reggie added their own wishes for a lifetime of love and happiness. After that, the waiters began taking their orders, and conversation, punctuated by frequent bursts of laughter, flowed easily throughout the room.

Erin and Nina were comparing the merits of the different spa treatments they'd received that morning when Nina spotted Megan making her way to their end of the table just as the bride-to-be said, "That wax girl was very thorough. Maybe a little too thorough. I'm still stinging in places where hair has no business growing."

"Where's that, Erin?" Megs asked. The

youngster stood at Erin's elbow and wore a perplexed expression.

Though the bride's eyes widened a tad, she didn't miss a beat. "In my nose!" she exclaimed. To sell her claim, Erin grabbed her own nose and gave it a good tweak.

Though Megs gave Erin a look that bordered on disbelief, she thrust a small slate into Nina's hands. The handwritten menu provided guests with a variety of options. "What are you getting?" the preteen demanded.

"Shrimp 'n' grits," Nina replied without hesitation. The dish was one of her favorites, and she considered Charlie's version the best of the best.

Megs turned up her nose. "Is there anything *good* on there?" She pointed a bright blue nail at the menu.

"Are you and Lily having trouble finding something you like?" Nina gave the girl a sympathetic look.

"Not Lily. She's in heaven. She wants something called bool-ya-base." Megs practically sneered. "Dimella's having it, too. Whatever it is."

"It's a fancy word for fish stew." From the time she'd spent overseeing the Happy Dolphin's kitchen, Nina knew the dish would include chunks of fresh lobster, jumbo shrimp and sea scallops in a rich broth.

"Whatev." Megs rolled her eyes. "Lily swears she's wanted it 'for her whole life.' Like she does all the time. Me? I just want a burger and fries. Or chicken nuggets."

Hmmm. The upscale menu was a little short on kid fare, but Charlie and Viola had two teens of their own. Nina had every confidence in her friend, the chef. He wouldn't let Zeke's daughter go hungry. "Tell you what, you let your waiter know exactly what you want, and he'll bring you something that'll knock your socks off."

Megs glanced down at her freshly polished toenails. "I'm not wearing socks," she said.

"Right." Nina smothered a smile while, beside her, Erin choked on a sip of water. "It's an expression. It means you'll be surprised…in a good way."

Megs heaved a sigh that sounded more like it should come from a thirty-year-old than a girl who stood on the cusp of her teenage years, but she tucked the menu under her arm and returned to her chair.

"You were so good with her," Erin observed while she blotted a few droplets with her napkin. "I'm not sure I'd have the patience."

"Of course, you would. In fact, you already

do," Nina pointed out. "You take her fishing and kayaking all the time. She loves hanging out with you."

Erin shook her head. The move sent tiny bands of color dancing across the table as the jewels on her ball cap caught and reflected the light. "That's different. When we're out on the water, we're doing something she loves. She knows she has to be nice or we'll head back in."

"Megs is a good girl," Nina said, watching as the child spoke with the waiter. "She reminds me of us when we were that age." She paused, not sure she would have been able to make a special request on her own when she was that young. "Maybe a little more worldly-wise than we were."

"Oh gosh." Erin smiled broadly. "Those were the days, weren't they? We were all going to marry little Bobby Warren and have a bazillion babies."

They fell silent for a moment while their waiter placed a bread basket and tiny pot of cheese dip in front of them.

"Do you ever wish you had?" Nina asked, when he'd moved on. It was almost embarrassing how gaga they'd all been over the boy who'd led the Little League team to the state championship.

"Married Bobby Warren?" When Erin shook her head this time, the color bands did a livelier dance. "Nah. He was a jerk. He'd hold my hand one day, yours the next and move on to Michelle by the end of the week."

"Not that," Nina corrected. "The other thing. Do you ever wish you'd had a baby?"

"Oh." Erin stilled for a moment before she cupped one hand over her ear and listened. "Hear that?" she asked.

"I don't hear a thing, other than everybody having a good time," Nina confessed.

"Neither do I. My biological clock never even started ticking."

"Ha!" Nina said as she followed her friend's reasoning. "Mine, either."

"It's really kind of a shame when you stop to think of it," Erin's voice dropped. "You and I never wanted children, but Reggie did. In the worst way. If there was ever someone who was born to be a mom, she's the one. But—" Erin shrugged. "It wasn't in the cards for her."

"She's got Hope now, though," Nina pointed out. "The way she fusses over that baby, you'd think Reggie had given birth to her." They'd all taken turns entertaining the toddler at the spa. Now she slept in her stroller, her hands and arms splayed out, the picture of contentment.

164

Erin glanced down the table at her sister and smiled. "Yeah. Hope's a cutie. And who knows? If she and Chris tie the knot, maybe one day…"

"Wait." In the middle of spreading some of the dip on a fragrant onion roll, Nina stilled. "I thought Reggie couldn't…"

Erin's eyes filled with a measured look. "The doctors never said whose fault it was." She sniffed. "Stranger things have happened. We've all heard about women who finally adopt and then, poof, they're pregnant."

"Huh. That's definitely something to think about." Nina finished with the spread and took a small bite. "Assuming Reggie and Chris are really serious about each other," she said when she'd swallowed.

"Oh, I think they are. I've never seen my sister as happy as she is when she's with Chris. I'm pretty sure he thinks she hung the moon."

"I guess we'll have to wait and see what happens," Nina mused.

Just then, their food began to arrive. As she'd suspected they would, Charlie and his staff had outdone themselves. She gave her own dish five stars and watched as the other women raved about the food they'd ordered. At the opposite end of the table, Megs's eyes grew round as saucers when her waiter placed a towering triple cheeseburger before her. Nina laughed silently while she watched the youngster figure out a plan of attack and put it into play by carefully dividing the meal into smaller sections. Meanwhile, despite Lily's declaration that her bouillabaisse was "the best ever," the ten-year-old lost interest in the spicy stew after only a few bites. Later, when Nina happened to glance their way again, she noted that both Lily and Dimella were happily helping Megs devour the burger and the mountain of fries that had accompanied it.

As the party began to wind down, Viola took the girls to the ladies' room. Reggie tended to Hope, who'd woken from her nap. Ashley dragged a spare chair closer to Nina and Erin.

"How'd it go with Lily at the spa?" Nina asked. She knew Zeke would want a full report.

"Great. We had the works—mini massages, mani-pedis, facials." The young woman laughed. "Lily enjoyed it all, although she called our facials a waste of perfectly good cucumbers."

Nina snorted. "That's Lily. She's a cook, through and through."

Ashley propped one elbow on the table. "You know, this is the first Christmas we aren't going to spend at our old house." Christmas dinner at the Robinsons' had been a tradition that stretched back to the year when Michelle was pregnant with the twins. "I thought I'd feel sad about that, but with everyone here, in a lot of ways, it feels the same. Can you believe Christmas is only three days away?"

Erin adjusted her bedazzled ball cap. "Only three more days till my wedding, you mean," she said, pulling a pouty face.

"Hey," Nina interrupted. "I know this is your bachelorette party, but not everything is about you." She gave her friend a good-natured shove. "Remember? We're all going to celebrate Christmas in the morning. I'm making the sweet rolls, same as I do every year. We'll get Reggie to sit under the tree and be Santa's elf, like she always does. Someone will throw away a gift card, and we'll spend an hour going through the wrapping paper in the recycling bin trying to find it."

Ashley grinned. "That's usually Aaron."

"Once that's all done, then comes the wedding."

Erin folded her arms across her chest. "I don't know why I can't just sleep in. After all, it is my wedding day." Despite the teasing glint in her eyes that told everyone she was just kidding, she continued her lament. "Ron and I agreed not to buy each other anything—the trip to the Keys will be our big present to ourselves. And the four of us don't exchange gifts." Michelle, Reggie, Nina and Erin had declared a moratorium on Christmas and birthday gifts a decade earlier. "Since I won't have anything under the tree, I should be allowed to sleep in," she argued.

"And miss out on Hope's first real Christmas?" The baby had only been a few weeks old this time last year. "Besides," Nina said cagily. "I wouldn't be too sure about that no present thing. There might be one box with your name on it."

"What is it?" Erin demanded.

Nina and Ashley traded sly glances. Michelle's daughter had been sworn to secrecy like the rest of them. They were all anxious to see Erin's face when she and Ron saw their surprise gift.

Refusing to divulge any more information, Nina tapped her knife against her glass to signal the final toast. It was time to round everyone up and get back on the bus. According to a text Zeke had sent earlier, the guys had landed a boatload of redfish and were planning a fish fry.

Ten

Reggie

C ontent beneath the red-and-white striped hat that identified her as Santa's helper, Reggie propped her hands on the floor behind her and leaned against them. She surveyed the happy faces of friends and family and soon-to-be family who'd gathered in the inn's living room. A happy sigh coursed through her. This was the kind of Christmas she'd always dreamed of having. Not one where Sam glowered in a corner, put out because he'd been forced to attend the festivities. Or one that Erin spent in some corner of the world so remote she couldn't even call home. But a Christmas filled with light and love and laughter. With a baby in the center of everything.

Her heart melted as Hope tore the wrapping

paper off yet another present. Before he left the apartment this morning, Chris had dressed his daughter in the white body shirt and green ruffled leggings Reggie had bought for the little girl. A matching green headband and a big, floppy bow kept the baby's blond curls out of her eyes and looked adorable on her. Not that Hope would wear the outfit for much longer. Even now, drool dampened the front of her cotton shirt. She'd be due for a change of clothes by the time she needed a new diaper. Fortunately, Reggie had anticipated that and had purchased an assortment of Christmassy outfits for the little one, including a frilly red-and-green plaid dress for her to wear to the wedding.

While Hope jingled the set of large plastic keys she'd unwrapped, Reggie drank in the sights and smells of the holiday. Red balls, streamers and lights decorated the regal balsam fir that stood at the center of the room where they'd all gathered to exchange gifts. Boughs of cut pine graced the top of the mantel. Up and down the staircase, shiny red ribbons held fragrant garlands in place. The twins had given each other cologne for Christmas, and Aaron had splashed some on his cheeks. The spicy tang blended, not unpleasantly, with the hot florals of Ashley's favorite fragrance. The aroma of Nina's

Christmas morning treats—one pan with orange filling, another with cinnamon—still drifted in the air, though Reggie was absolutely certain not so much as a scrap of the yummy yeast rolls remained.

Sitting cross-legged on the floor, she felt the gentle nudge of Chris's elbow at her side. Her attention shifted to the man who occupied more and more of her heart with every passing day.

"She's done with that one," he said, lifting his chin to indicate his daughter.

Sure enough, Hope had abandoned the shiny plastic keys. Instead, she held a scrap of wrapping paper, which she studied intently as she wiggled one edge back and forth.

"Ready to see what else Santa brought you?" Crawling over to the baby, Reggie bopped the little girl lightly on the nose with the green pom-pom that dangled from the end of her elf cap.

"San," Hope said. Dropping the paper, she held out her hands. Her pudgy fingers opened and closed in a classic "gimme" motion.

A click sounded. From the other side of the room, Aaron gave a thumbs-up sign. He'd captured the moment with his digital camera.

"It didn't take her long to get the hang of unwrapping gifts, did it?" Sitting beside Erin, Ron chuckled. He and his fiancée had decided the whole can't-see-the-bride-on-her-wedding-day thing was nothing more than superstitious bunk. He'd knocked on the back door just as Nina was taking the sweet rolls out of the oven this morning, and no one had had the heart to make him leave.

"About two seconds," Chris agreed. "She's gonna put me in the poorhouse, that one."

The comment sent good-natured laughter rippling through the room.

Reggie scrambled under the tree, where she grabbed one of the three remaining presents. This one contained her gift to Hope, and she whispered a silent prayer that she'd gotten something the little girl would like more than the box she'd put it in. Although she had to admit, this particular box was pretty. Instead of wrapping it in paper destined for the recycling bin, she'd spent hours painting snowmen and Christmas trees on the plain cardboard. She placed it in front of the baby while Chris whisked away the remnants of the last gift.

Hope scratched at the box, obviously perplexed by the lack of paper to tear.

"It's okay, honey," Reggie coaxed. "You just take the cover off this one." She lifted one corner of the colorful lid and let it drop. "Peep eye," she teased.

"Peep." Hope's little fingers dug for purchase on the corner. It took her a moment, but she grabbed hold. Instead of letting the lid fall as Reggie had done, though, she knocked the cover to one side. Nestled in a bed of white tissue paper inside the box lay a baby doll with blond hair and big blue eyes like Hope's. The little girl breathed in sharply. "Bay," she whispered.

"That's right," Reggie said. "It's a baby doll. She's your baby."

Hope snatched the doll out of the box and clutched it to her chest. "Bay," she said again.

"Well, I think that's a home run." Chris's observation and his smile warmed Reggie all the way to her toes.

"One more present?" she asked the baby.

Still pressing her new "Bay" close, Hope made the gimme sign with her free hand.

"Okay, sweetheart." Diving under the tree, Reggie retrieved the child's final gift. Chris had wrapped this one himself using brightly colored paper that showed cartoon Santas driving sleighs and dancing with elves. Reggie pushed the lumpy shape in front of the child. Still holding her baby doll, Hope sat and stared at it for several seconds. At last, she wrenched her gaze off the present long enough to give her daddy a look.

"Want some help?" Chris scooted to his daughter's side, where he made a show of tearing a long strip of the wrapping paper. Hope giggled and grabbed the loose flap. She tugged, and the hole widened enough to reveal a pink-and-white riding toy.

"Oh," she cooed.

Reggie put a little extra effort into remaining upbeat when Hope lost interest in her doll.

"What to go for a ride?" Chris ripped away the rest of the paper. He picked the baby up and set her in the seat. "Here we go," he sang. "Vroom, vroom." Gently, he rocked the car forward a few inches and back again.

Hope blinked as if she wasn't sure whether to laugh or cry.

"Oh, what fun!" Reggie swallowed her own reservations. Clapping her hands to her cheeks, she summoned her happiest grin and let her eyes go wide.

As she'd hoped the baby would do, Hope took her cue from Reggie's antics. The toddler giggled. "Go," she cried, and Chris repeated the motion along with the appropriate sounds.

"Up." She held out her arms.

Her meaning was perfectly clear. Chris lifted the little girl and set her down on her feet. He hovered in case she fell, but Hope had been walking unassisted for a couple of months and quickly found her balance. Much to Reggie's delight, the little girl toddled over to the baby doll. Grabbing it, she took it to the car, where she dropped it unceremoniously onto the seat and gave the toy a shove. Her face lit up when the car glided forward. She giggled happily while Chris and Reggie laughed.

"Did you give Bay a ride?" Reggie asked.

"Go." Hope pushed the car and giggled. "Go."

"Well, I guess that's about it," Erin announced after they'd watched Hope play with her new toys until the baby climbed into Chris's lap for a rest. "If y'all will excuse me, I'm going upstairs. I heard a rumor about a wedding this evening."

"Hold on there just a few more minutes," Michelle cautioned when Erin started to rise. "There's one more present under the tree."

Immediately, a hush fell over the room. The silence made Reggie painfully aware of the rustle of pine needles, the tinkle of ornaments when she reached behind the tree stand for the package she'd deliberately overlooked earlier. One of the branches snagged her hat, knocking it askew. Retrieving the small, wrapped present, she sat up. With the gift in her lap, she straightened her pom-pom.

"Oh, for the love of…" Nina breathed. "Hurry up."

"Okay, okay." Reggie pretended to grumble. She peered at the tag as if she couldn't make out the writing. "This one's addressed to—" Squinting, she held the box up to the light. "Hmmmm. Would you imagine that? This one's for Ron and Erin from, um, from Santa." She held the present out to her sister.

"I thought we agreed not to exchange gifts," Erin said. Her lips pressed together.

"This one's special," Michelle explained. "It's from all of us." She gestured to the entire group. Everyone in the room had contributed to the project in some way, including Edwina, who'd crocheted a cozy afghan for the newlyweds' couch. Ashley had helped Michelle and Reggie with the decorating, while Aaron and his trusty camera had documented their efforts.

Giddy excitement rushed through Reggie. She saw the same anticipation reflected on Michelle and Nina's faces.

Erin handed the box to Ron. "It's for both of us. You should open it."

Ron slipped one finger under the tape. He pried it up before carefully starting to unfold the corners.

"This is going to take forever," Nina complained.

"Just go ahead and rip it, honey," Erin said sweetly.

"Oooooh!" the group murmured when Ron peeled back the paper to reveal a wooden box.

"Daddy, did you do this?" Erin pointed to the set of wedding rings someone had carved into the lid.

"Yes, baby." Frank nodded. He squeezed his wife's hand. Knowing Reggie and Erin's father had taken up woodworking after he'd retired, Michelle had asked him to create the box.

"It's pretty, Dad. You're really getting good at this." Still, confusion knitted Erin's brows as she scanned the room. "Um? Thank you?" she said, obviously not quite certain why everyone was so excited over a jewelry box.

"There's something inside. Open it," Reggie urged.

"If you insist." Erin shrugged. While Ron held onto the base, she removed the lid. She plucked something from inside and held up two keys that dangled from the fob Reggie had crafted to match the sign on the door to the inn's newest suite.

"Oasis?" Ron read the letters burned into the small piece of driftwood. "Isn't that the name of the honeymoon suite Zeke was putting in the turret?"

"Waaait," Erin breathed. "Is this what I think it is?"

"Why don't you take a look?" Michelle suggested. The knowing smile that tugged on her lips ruined her innocent expression.

"You guys…" Erin stood.

"You want to tell me what's going on?" Ron stared up at his bride.

"C'mon." The ring on her finger sparkled as Erin motioned toward the other side of the house. "Let's go see."

Reggie tilted her head toward Chris, who sat with a sleepy Hope in his lap. "You go ahead," he said. "I'll stay here with her."

Anxious to see her sister's reaction to their surprise, Reggie joined Michelle and Nina behind Ron and Erin as the couple race-walked through the house. Reggie's parents, along with Ashley and Aaron, followed them in and out of the living room. At the end of the short hall that led to a private entrance to the turret, Erin stood back while Ron slipped one of the keys into the lock and twisted the doorknob. The door swung open onto a furnished suite that lived up to its name.

Pale yellow walls turned the once dark and gloomy turret into a warm and inviting retreat. Solid hardwood floors and trim, along with green accents, added color to the décor. A jute rug defined the living area, where a hunter-green sofa and two chairs covered in a striped print provided seating. Barstools clustered around the island Zeke had built to separate the main area from a compact but well-designed kitchen. In the recessed niche, the spiral staircase led to a second-floor loft where there was more than adequate space for the king-size bed, dresser and nightstands.

"Oh, my heart," Erin cried. She pressed one hand to her chest, another to her mouth. "Is this… You didn't… How?" Tears dampened her cheeks when she spun to face the others. "What have you done?" she asked, breathless.

"I think that means she likes it," Reggie said to Michelle and Nina as she swept her sister into a one-armed embrace. Reaching out, Erin grasped Ron's hand while the others joined them in a group hug.

"You and Ron can stay here until you find the perfect piece of property and have your own house built," Michelle explained. "It's away from the rest of the inn, so you'll have as much privacy as you want."

"There are enough meals for two in the freezer to get you through a month," Nina added. "I made all your favorite dishes."

"You have great views from the upstairs windows," Reggie pointed out.

Erin plucked a couple of tissues from a box someone had thoughtfully left on the kitchen counter. She blotted her eyes and cheeks. "I thought we agreed to turn this into a honeymoon suite," she said through her tears.

"Reggie, Nina and I overruled that idea. We decided that you and Ron needed an apartment more." Michelle shrugged. "With a little paint, a bearskin rug and a few changes here and there, it won't be any trouble to switch things up once you and Ron move into your own place."

"What? We don't get a bearskin rug? I like those." Slipping one arm around Erin's waist, Ron gave his wife-to-be a lascivious wink.

"Oh, you!" Erin tapped his shoulder play-fully, but Reggie saw the warm glow in her sister's eyes. The two were made for each other, and knowing that filled her with joy.

Michelle coughed politely. "Um, let's make sure you like what we did do to the place." She led the couple on a brief tour.

When he and Erin had thoroughly inspected every nook and cranny and pronounced the apartment "absolutely perfect," Ron cleared his throat. Addressing the entire group, he said, "I can't thank you enough for all this. We've looked at dozens of rentals. They were either hideously expensive or, well, they just wouldn't do. Nellie said we might have to get something in Destin and commute back and forth."

"We didn't want to be that far away from everyone." Erin reached for Michelle and Nina's hands and gave them a squeeze.

"Or waste that much time driving back and forth," Ron added. To give the clients of his fishing charter business the best experience, he needed to be on the water by sunup.

"Speaking of time," Reggie said with a glance at the clock on the kitchen's built-in microwave. "What say we leave this for now—it'll be here, ready and waiting for you to move into when you get back from the Keys. For now, we have a wedding to get ready for. The stylist will be here in an hour for hair and makeup, and we don't want to keep her waiting."

Nothing could delay this wedding, she added silently. Tonight, when her sister and Ron said their vows, they'd embark on a second chance at love and happiness. And if it happened for them, it might happen for her, too.

Someday.

Eleven

Erin

The scrape of something heavy being moved across the floor followed a solid *thunk* that came from somewhere downstairs.

"What's going on down there?" With a tissue tucked around her neck to keep her makeup from rubbing off on her robe, Erin strode toward the door of the spacious Tarpon suite. Used to bouncing from one place to another, she hadn't minded moving into the set of rooms at the top of the stairs after a water pipe burst at Chris's place. Especially since the roomy sitting room was large enough to double as a bridal suite on her wedding day.

"Whoa! Hold up. You can't go out there."

Reggie turned away from the mirror, where she'd been fussing over the updo the stylist had given her. She slipped in front of Erin and blocked her path to the door.

"Why not?" Erin peered over her sister's shoulder. Not that it did any good. Last time she checked, she didn't have the X-ray vision she'd need to see through solid wood. Any more than she had the gift of sight and could predict the future.

Doubt swirled in her stomach. Her fingers shook. Was marrying Ron the right thing? Was it too late to call off the wedding?

"Let's just say the Oasis wasn't the only surprise we have in store for you today." Reggie wiggled her eyebrows.

Her sister's playful gesture fell flat. Despite her best efforts, Erin's voice turned shrill. "And I don't get any say in the matter?"

Another loud scrape confirmed that someone was moving heavy furniture around. The news wasn't one bit reassuring. She shot a questioning look at Michelle and Nina. "Didn't anyone tell you it's not a good idea to pull tricks on the bride on her wedding day? I've half a mind to cancel the wedding."

"Simmer down, now," Nina soothed. "That's

just your nerves talking. You've been looking forward to this day for months. Everything is going to be fine."

"But they're rearranging furniture," Erin protested. She and Ron hadn't wanted a big to-do. A simple exchange of vows in front of the fireplace would suit them just fine. Okay, maybe a small part of her had wanted to walk down the long center aisle of the First Baptist Church like her mom suggested, but the same minister would officiate. That had to count for something, didn't it? She had a beautiful dress and her three best friends as her attendants. Wasn't that enough?

Apparently not, judging from what was going on below them.

"Listen. No one's doing anything too crazy. We're just making things a wee bit nicer." Michelle pinched her thumb and forefinger together. "Ashley and Sara are in charge down there, and Ron is helping. You trust them, don't you?"

"I guess." Erin slipped one foot in and out of her slipper. "I'm just"—she took a breath and tried to ignore the way it shuddered in her chest—"nervous."

Michelle laughed softly. "Cold feet. Every bride gets them. Remember the day Allan and I got married? I was wound up tighter than that grandfather clock in the living room. Turned out I was worried for nothing. We had twenty-five wonderful years together."

"Not me," Reggie said. "I wasn't nervous at all the day I married Sam. Huh." She shrugged. "Maybe getting a little worked up on your wedding day is a good sign."

Her friends were right, as usual. Slowly, Erin felt the knot in her stomach unfurl. She took another breath, and when more loud noises drifted up the stairs, she didn't flinch. She did, however, have questions. "How's everything else going? The cake? The flowers? Dinner?"

"Fine. Fine. And fine," Nina said. "The cake is absolutely perfect—Viola really outdid herself this time." Her assistant cook might not be classically trained, but her cakes were tasty works of art.

Michelle drank from her water bottle. "Polly delivered the floral arrangements. White roses, just what you asked for."

"Dinner is well underway. Ethan and Viola have everything under control in the kitchen." Nina flipped a loose strand over one shoulder. She'd opted to leave her hair down for the ceremony. "We have a little bit of time yet before we help you into your dress. Do you have everything you need? Something borrowed?"

"Mom lent me the diamond solitaire Daddy gave her for their fortieth anniversary." Erin slid the pendant back and forth on the gold chain around her neck. "I have a copper penny to go in my shoe; it doubles as my something old. For blue..." She crossed to the dresser and opened the top drawer. "I have a little something for each of you."

"I thought we said no presents." Reggie frowned.

"We said no *Christmas* presents." Erin addressed her sister's reflection in the mirror. "These are *wedding* presents."

She retrieved the three Tiffany-blue boxes tied with white ribbons. The gifts were all the same, but she'd written a personal note to each of her friends and her sister. She'd wanted her younger sibling to know how much she appreciated how Reggie had forced her to take a hard look at her feelings for Ron. Because of that, she'd known it was the right decision when she gave him—gave them—a second chance. Nina had encouraged her to examine her motives for settling down after the two decades she'd spent traveling the globe. It had given her the assurance she'd needed to tell Ron she'd "been there, done that" when he asked her to go away with him. Michelle's steadfast faith that true love would find a way had helped her eliminate all her other doubts one by one.

She tapped her toe while they opened their gifts.

"Oh, it's beautiful," Reggie said, holding up the gold bracelet made of cockle shells and graceful dolphins surrounding a teardrop of blue sea glass.

"Thank you so much," Nina gushed. She lay the bracelet across her thin wrist and worked the lobster clasp. "It's all right if we wear them today, isn't it?"

"I was hoping you would." Erin extended her hand. The same delicate bracelet circled her own wrist. "It's my 'something new and blue,'" she explained. "And a token of our friendship."

All of a sudden, she felt weepy. She took a breath to steady herself. "I know marrying Ron is right, but I hate the thought of us drifting apart. I don't know what I'd do if I didn't have you all in my life." Deep breathing wasn't going to cut it. She needed Kleenex, pronto.

Reliable as always, Michelle was there, tissues in hand. "Here, take these," she ordered. "And have some water. If you cry, your mascara will run."

Nina unscrewed the cap on a fresh bottle and handed it across. "Drink up," she coached.

It took a minute, but Erin calmed. She sank onto a nearby wingback chair. Reggie, Michelle and Erin shuffled their own chairs until the four of them sat, knees touching, in a tight circle.

"Now," Michelle said when they were settled, "just because you're getting married, that doesn't mean our friendship will fade. One thing has nothing to do with the other."

"Yeah," Reggie agreed. "You'll always be my sister, but you're my friend, too. That's not going to change once you say 'I do.' We stuck together after I married Sam, didn't we?" She held out her hands, palms up.

"We've been blessed to spend the better part of a year together, living in one house, working toward one goal," Nina said. "It's made our friendship stronger, but it wasn't always that way. Michelle was a stay-at-home mom with two children. Reggie and Sam lived on the other side of town. I bounced around from job to job, apartment to apartment. You spent a lot of time in places none of the rest of us have ever been."

Not exactly sure what point Nina was making, Erin let her confusion show.

"What I'm saying is, it doesn't matter whether we're in one place or scattered across the globe. Whether we're single or married or something in between."

"Things are going to change." Michelle crowded closer. "That's part of life. None of us can predict where we'll be or what we'll be doing ten years from now. But wherever we are or whatever is going on in our lives, our friendship will endure."

"To put it bluntly," Reggie piped in, "we've got each other's back. Now and in the future."

Erin sniffed and, careful not to smudge her makeup, blotted her nose. Reggie and her friends were right. Their bonds were stronger now than they'd ever been. Nothing—not new husbands or new jobs or new life goals—was going to change that. "I love you," she said simply. Reaching out, she grasped the hands of the three people she'd always trust to be in her corner, just as she'd be in theirs.

She didn't know how long they sat together, their heads nearly touching, their hands entwined. A minute? Two? The moment might have lasted longer, but a knock at the door signaled an end to it.

"Erin?" Ashley's familiar voice came from the hall. "Aaron wants to know if this is a good time to take some pictures of your bridal party."

"Um…" Her voice dropped to a whisper. "Is it that time already?" she asked. She and Michelle were still in their dressing gowns. Nina wore chef's pants and a loose tunic, while Reggie sported a T-shirt and jogging pants. Her eyes widened. "We're not even dressed yet."

"Give us about fifteen, Ash," her mom called. "The bride's almost ready."

And, thanks to her friends, Erin knew it was true.

While Peabo Bryson and Regina Belle's rendition of "A Whole New World" poured from hidden speakers, Reggie slowly descended the wide, curving staircase that led to the living room. When she was halfway down, Nina began her descent. Michelle gave Erin a final hug before she joined the procession.

Left alone on the upstairs landing, Erin shifted with nervous energy. During last night's practice, she'd remained completely out of sight until the song ended and the music changed to "The Wedding March." Tonight, though, she was too eager for her first glimpse of what waited below. Expecting to see a few friends and family scattered about the living room on sofas and chairs while the bridal party gathered at the front of the room, she edged close enough to the banister to steal a peek.

But instead of an informal gathering with a few long-stemmed white roses in bud vases here and there, rows of white chairs spread out on either side of a red runner dotted with white petals. Baskets containing masses of white roses stood at various spots along the aisle. Candles flickered on the mantel and from a pair of tall candelabra that flanked an honest-to-gosh podium. Dave, Zeke and Chris, looking extraordinarily handsome in black suits and ties, formed a line to right of the minister.

The effect was stunning and exactly the simple elegance Erin had wanted, only more so. She bowed her head and whispered a quiet thanks that she'd been blessed with friends who understood her wants and desires even more than she did herself.

One by one, Reggie, Nina and Michelle glided down the stairs. Reaching the foot of the staircase, they slowly walked up the aisle and took their places on the left. As they did, the expressions on the men softened. Watching their eyes light up, Erin wondered how long it would be before her sister and their friends each vowed to love, honor and cherish the men who stood beside the minister tonight. She had no doubt whatsoever that Zeke was head over heels in love with Nina. Chris only had eyes for Reggie and she him, while Dave was totally smitten with Michelle and had been from the moment they met.

The song came to an end. The opening bars of "The Wedding March" played. Chairs creaked and clothing rustled as their guests rose and turned toward the staircase. Erin stepped onto the first tread, where she paused for a long second to let her gaze travel over the people below. She smiled brightly at Charlie and Viola who, along with Dimella and Malcom, were watching over Hope. Ashley and Sara stood together in one row. She couldn't see Aaron's face behind the digital camera he aimed in her direction but made a special note to thank them for all they'd done to make this day extra special. Ethan and several of the staff stood off to one side dressed in the dark pants and white shirts they'd wear when they served dinner later. Her focus shifted to her parents. Her dad beamed while her mom blotted her eyes with a tissue. Edwina's warm smile told Erin not to worry; her mom's tears were happy ones.

Movement up front caught her attention as Ron took his place beside the minister. Her breath caught. Everything else faded from view as she and Ron locked eyes. His grew misty. Tears welled in hers. Mindful of her mascara, she blinked rapidly, but her focus didn't waver. A certainty she had never known before settled solidly in her chest. It stamped out the last vestiges of every doubt.

Ron was the only man for her. He always had been. They'd lost precious time together because of decisions they'd made when they were young and foolish, but those days were behind them. Now they looked forward to a future filled with happiness and love.

Her heart light, she floated down the rest of the stairs, eager to exchange vows with the man she loved and begin the second chapter of their lives together.

Epilogue

Michelle

*M*ichelle ran her fingers over the cover of the cushion on her favorite rattan chair. The cloth felt worn to the touch. In places, it had visibly thinned, almost to the point of fraying. She made a mental note to start looking for fabric to replace the cushions that had seen a lot of use over the past five years. Maybe stripes this time instead of florals.

Dave emerged from the house with a small serving tray that held a bowl of carrot and celery sticks as well as a tub of hummus. Ice and orange liquid sloshed gently in the pitcher he carried. He glanced at the horizon, where the setting sun had set the sky ablaze. "It never gets old, does it?"

"Never," Michelle agreed. She leaned forward, taking the weight of the heavy pitcher from him.

Dave had tweaked his back the week before playing tennis, and although he swore he was no longer in pain, it made little sense for him to push his limits. Especially not with the four-day getaway they had planned for next weekend.

"Are the last of the guests gone?" he asked as he placed the lighter tray on the coffee table beside an array of sodas and bottles of water.

"All checked out. The girls are cleaning their rooms as we speak." Jocelyn and Carol had been part of the housekeeping staff almost from Day One. Michelle trusted them to leave the hardwood floors gleaming and the bathroom fixtures glistening.

"Have I ever told you how much I look forward to everyone getting together on Sunday evenings?" Dave asked while Michelle poured some of the Gulf Coast Sunset into two of the glasses she'd brought out earlier. She handed one to him and kept the other for herself.

"You might have mentioned it once or twice." She smiled at their running joke. She and her friends had decided early on that they wouldn't accept new reservations for Sundays. Though the inn rarely emptied out completely, the guests who stayed past the weekend had already learned the ropes and rarely required much of her time or attention.

"Where is everyone?" Erin, Nina and Reggie and assorted spouses and children usually joined them for drinks and snacks before the start of a new week.

"Erin and Ron will be along in a few minutes. He was a little late coming back from a deep-sea charter. He's bringing us a piece of smoked snapper for supper," Michelle answered. Four years earlier, the couple had purchased the property next door. The house they'd built was just a short walk away.

Dave rubbed his hands together. "Can't wait. That little smokehouse of his is doing a booming business." Once his charter service was on steady legs, Ron had had a long talk with Gus before erecting a second smokehouse in Sugar Sand Beach. By mutual agreement, Ron only smoked the fish his clients caught. In return, he kept a share of the finished product, most of which Gus sold for him at the grocery store.

"Reggie and Chris will be a little bit later, but they'll be here." Michelle smiled softly. "They're waiting for Matthew to wake up from his nap."

Dave's face lit. "I'm glad. I've been saving up a few knock-knock jokes for Hope." The six-year-old loved nothing better than sharing jokes and puns with anyone who'd listen. More often than not, that person was Dave. Though none of their three children seemed like they were in any hurry to get married, he took the role of grandfather-in-training quite seriously.

"Matthew's growing so fast," Michelle commented. "Reggie says he's a good baby, but they're still dead on their feet most of the time. Although he did sleep through the night for the first time this week."

"Our little miracle baby," Dave mused. "After all she went through with her first husband, it's good to see Reggie so happy."

"Chris, too. I think he counted every minute of the pregnancy. I've never seen a man as nervous as he was when Reggie went into labor." She paused to savor the memory of Chris's face when he stepped beyond the swinging doors into the labor-and-delivery waiting room to share the good news that mother and son were fine. "He went down on his knees right then and there and gave thanks."

"We all joined him," Dave said, remembering. Between him and Ron and Zeke, they'd worn a path in the waiting room's carpet. "What about Nina?"

Michelle waved a hand. "She'll be on her way as soon as Megs's choir practice ends. Can you believe she's singing a solo at church next weekend? I'd be so nervous, I'd probably forget the words." In Virginia, Michelle had sung in the church choir for a number of years. Once she'd moved to Sugar Sand Beach, though, she'd been content with her seat in the third row of the First Baptist Church. Especially when Dave sat beside her.

"Megs has a lovely voice. She'll do fine. She owned the stage in the talent contest, didn't she?" They'd all turned out for the high school event and cheered as the teenager took first place.

"Yeah." Dave was right, of course. If Megs could nail a Jason Mraz song in front of hundreds of her peers, she'd bring everyone in church to tears next week.

"But what I want to know is, has Nina forgiven Lily?" Dave swirled the ice in his glass and took a sip.

Michelle chuckled. In typical teenage fashion, the tiny blonde had announced over dinner last month that she'd "gone green." She'd refused to eat Nina's ham-and-cheese crepes that night, and in the three weeks since, the chef had struggled with her stepdaughter's new diet regimen. "Did you try some of that bread she made?" she asked.

"Uh, no. I'm all for eating healthy," Dave said as he snagged a carrot, "but I draw the line at nuts and sprouts pasted together with coconut oil."

"Be glad you didn't. It was nasty." Michelle made a face. "Nina's been upset about it, but I told her not to fret. In another month, Lily will get tired of juicing her own beets and carrots and she'll be on to the next food fad."

"That's teenagers for you. Personally, I'm glad Sara's well past that stage." Dave stretched his long legs.

"Have you heard from her this week?"

"She says everything is on track for her appointment." Dave's pride in his daughter's accomplishments shone in his eyes. Sara had made the short list for an appointment to the bench. "I thought we might have lunch with her on our way out next week. If that's all right with you."

"Of course, it is." Sara had welcomed her into the family with open arms. They spoke on the phone at least once a week. She'd no more pass up the opportunity to visit with Dave's daughter than she would with Aaron and Ashley.

Not that seeing either of the twins was even a remote possibility. Aaron had received a big promotion and was spending three years in the Philippines overseeing a project for CJX. While he was there, he'd earned his certification as a master diver. The underwater photos he texted to her were nothing short of incredible.

LEIGH DUNCAN

Meanwhile, Ashley had put her sorority experience to good use and had landed a job writing grant proposals after graduation. Recently, she'd gone into business for herself and, by all reports, was doing quite well. Well enough to buy a condo not far from their old neighborhood.

"Good. I'll ask Sara to meet us at Harry's around one." The restaurant in downtown Tallahassee was a favorite of theirs. Its location near the courthouse was an added plus. "We'll have plenty of time for a nice long chat before we hit the road again. It's only five hours from there down to the Treasure Coast." They'd spent their honeymoon at one of the area's ocean-front inns and had enjoyed their stay so much, he'd made reservations there for this trip. "Are you ready for our little getaway?"

"I can't wait," Michelle answered honestly. She looked up at the man she'd fallen a little more in love with every day since that day six years earlier when she'd walked into his office. Wanting to be absolutely sure, they'd taken their time before setting a date. After that, there'd been prenups to sign, and they'd given their kids plenty of time to get used to the idea. But eventually, the big day had arrived. She'd basked in Dave's love ever since and he hers.

Still, they did lead busy lives. The upcoming long weekend would be the first break they'd taken since their honeymoon. Four whole glorious days alone together couldn't come fast enough. "It's lovely there," she said.

"I always enjoy the differences between the Atlantic and the Gulf. More waves. More shells. And who knows, maybe we'll find a gold doubloon washed up on the shore this time."

"That'd be exciting!" The topic piqued Michelle's interest. Several Spanish ships had gone down off the coast of Florida in the 1700s. Some of them were loaded with treasure.

"Every few years, someone finds a coin or two. Might as well be us." Dave shrugged.

"As much fun as that would be, I'm really looking forward to spending some quality time with my new husband." She twined her fingers with Dave's when he reached for them. The rays of the sinking sun bounced off the white gold ring on her left hand. He wore a matching band on his.

"Oh, look." She shaded her eyes with her free hand. "Here come Erin and Ron now."

Walking close to each other, the couple crested the small hill that led past the sign that welcomed guests to the Sugar Sand Inn and Cafe.

A thrill of anticipation passed through

Michelle. "Nina's car just turned in at the gate. Reggie and Chris are right behind them."

Dave stirred. "I better put those appetizers in the oven." Chef Nina and her staff prepared trays of yummy morsels and left them in the freezer for their Sunday evening get-togethers.

"Thanks, hon." Michelle gave Dave a quick kiss.

As Dave headed for the kitchen, she rose and crossed to the railing that circled the porch. Five—no, nearly six—years ago, she and her friends had each arrived at separate crossroads in their lives. Instead of going off in different directions, they'd banded together to turn a long-abandoned house into a first-class inn. Eventually, they'd succeeded, though they'd faced some challenges along the way. They'd overcome them by relying on one another's strengths and, in doing so, each of them had been given a second chance at life, love and happiness.

Her heart full, Michelle waved a hearty welcome as the best friends a woman could ever want returned once more to the Sugar Sand Inn.

Thank you for reading
Christmas at Sugar Sand Inn!

Michelle, Reggie, Nina and Erin's heartwarming
story has come to an end, but Leigh is currently
working on another great series about friends
and family and fresh starts.

Sign up for Leigh's newsletter to get the
latest news about upcoming releases,
excerpts, and more!

https://leighduncan.com/newsletter/

Books by Leigh Duncan

SUGAR SAND BEACH SERIES

The Gift at Sugar Sand Inn
The Secret at Sugar Sand Inn
The Cafe at Sugar Sand Inn
The Reunion at Sugar Sand Inn
Christmas at Sugar Sand Inn

HEART'S LANDING SERIES

A Simple Wedding
A Cottage Wedding
A Waterfront Wedding

ORANGE BLOSSOM SERIES

Butterfly Kisses
Sweet Dreams

HOMETOWN HEROES SERIES

Luke
Brett
Dan
Travis
Colt
Garrett
The Hometown Heroes Collection, A Boxed Set

LEIGH DUNCAN

SINGLE TITLE BOOKS

A Country Wedding
Journey Back to Christmas
The Growing Season
Pattern of Deceit
Rodeo Daughter
His Favorite Cowgirl

NOVELLAS

The Billionaire's Convenient Secret
A Reason to Remember

Find all Leigh's books at:
leighduncan.com/books

Acknowledgements

Every book takes a team effort. I want to give special thanks to those who made *Christmas at Sugar Sand Inn* possible.

Cover design
Chris Kridler at
Sky Diary Productions

House photo used in cover illustration
Taken by Jerrye and Roy Klotz via Wikipedia,
licensed under Creative Commons
(link: https://creativecommons.org/licenses/by-sa/4.0/deed.en)

Editing Services
Chris Kridler at
Sky Diary Productions

Interior formatting
Amy Atwell and Team
Author E.M.S.

About the Author

Leigh Duncan is the award-winning author of more than two dozen novels, novellas and short stories. Though she started writing fiction at the tender age of six, she didn't get serious about writing a novel until her 40th birthday, and she offers all would-be authors this piece of advice: Don't wait so long!

Leigh sold her first, full-length novel in 2010. In 2017, she was thrilled when Hallmark Publishing chose her as the lead author for their new line of romances and cozy mysteries. A National Readers' Choice Award winner, an Amazon best-selling author and recently named a National Best-Selling author by Publisher's Weekly, Leigh lives on Florida's East Coast where she writes women's fiction and sweet, contemporary romance with a dash of Southern sass.

Want to get in touch with Leigh? She loves to hear from readers and fans. Visit leighduncan.com to send her a note. Join Leigh on Facebook, and don't forget to sign up for her newsletter so you get the latest news about fun giveaways, special offers or her next book!

About the Cover

The minute I came up with the idea of writing about four best friends who open a beach-side inn, I knew exactly which house I wanted to put on the covers of these books. With its gingerbread trim and Queen Anne-style architecture, the Wood/Spann house is easily one of the most beautiful homes I've ever seen. Built in 1895 by F.S. Wood, the house is a part of Troy, Alabama's College Street Historical District and is listed in the National Registry of Historic Places. Best of all, it belongs to a member of my very own family!

Aunt Betty, thank you so much for letting me feature your incredible home on the covers of the books in the Sugar Sand Beach series!

68140663R00130